COURAGE OF THE WITCH

WITCHES OF KEATING HOLLOW, BOOK 5

DEANNA CHASE

ABOUT THIS BOOK

Welcome to Keating Hollow, the enchanted town full of love, friendship, and family.

After Hanna Pelsh lost her sister over a decade ago, she vowed to live her life to the fullest. And she does just that. When she's not running the family coffee shop and volunteering her body to research for the mysterious disease that took her sister, Hanna dives head first into every adventure she can find. The only problem? The man she's loved since she was fifteen doesn't seem able to commit.

Rhys Silver has his dream job working at the Keating Hollow brewery. The only thing missing is a partner by his side. He's known who he wants for as long as he can remember. He also knows he's no good for her. But when the worst happens, he has a choice to make... overcome his fears or lose her forever.

CHAPTER 1

"*H*anna!" Faith Townsend yelled as she rushed into the Incantation Café. "I need a cupcake, STAT."

Hanna turned from the baking counter and spotted her friend mid-yawn, her eyes droopy with fatigue. Her pale hair was pulled back into a ponytail, but tendrils had escaped, making her look disheveled. "Goodness. Is *someone* keeping you up late at night or what?"

She let out an exasperated snort. "I wish that's why I was so beat. It would certainly make Hunter happy."

"Busy at the spa?" Hanna asked, handing her a red velvet cupcake with one hand and pouring the milk for her fully-leaded double latte with the other.

"Busy doesn't begin to cover it. Ever since Vivian started as a sales rep, we've been booked solid. If I don't get a second therapist in there soon, I'm going to drop from exhaustion."

"Got any promising prospects?" Hanna gathered up some day-old cookies for her best friend, wishing she could be more helpful. But it wasn't like she could just go lend a hand. Faith needed a trained therapist, not a baker who'd only ever worked at one place.

"Yes, thank the gods. I had someone inquire a few days ago, but she's coming in from out of town and can't make it until next week. I just hope she's as good in person as she is on paper, because if not, I'm going to have to hire the girl that smells like stinky cheese or the dude who winked at me no less than twenty times during his interview." Faith visibly shuddered at the thought.

Hanna chuckled as she finished up the latte and handed it to Faith.

"Thank you," Faith said, giving Hanna an exaggerated wink that made her laugh harder.

"You're welcome. Now go wrap someone in seaweed or scrub them down with coffee grounds or whatever witchcraft you wield over at A Touch of Magic."

"Next up is a salt scrub followed by a cupping treatment."

"Cupping treatment? That sounds dirty." She pushed the bag of cookies toward Faith. "Please tell me you haven't turned the place into one of those happy-ending spas."

Faith choked on her latte as she snorted out another laugh. "Stop," she said once she got herself under control. "Listen, can I take a raincheck on our girls' night tonight? I'll probably fall asleep in my stuffed trout."

"Sure, honey." Hanna gave her a gentle smile. "You get some rest. We can meet up this weekend or whenever you have time." She was careful to keep her tone light and full of understanding, but the truth was Hanna was disappointed. Faith had been leading a very full existence lately with her new business, a new man in her life who came with a young child, and a house that was being rebuilt. It was all good, but it didn't leave a lot of time for girls' night, and Hanna was missing her friend.

"I promise we'll get together in a few days. Just let me check with Hunter to coordinate schedules, okay? I'll text you."

"Okay." Hanna waved and gave her an encouraging smile as she rushed back out the door.

"That's too bad. I know you were looking forward to seeing her. I guess that means you're free tonight?" Mary Pelsh asked from the door of her office.

Hanna glanced over at her mother and shrugged. "Yeah, I guess. But it's okay. It gives me a chance to finish reading Robyn Peterman's latest release." Hanna smiled at her mom. "Her books are hilarious."

"Mmhmm. Sounds like a nice relaxing evening, but a girl your age should be out on the town on a Friday night."

Hanna suppressed a sigh. She was at the ripe old age of twenty-seven, and her mother was getting anxious about her love life. She had a feeling Mary was just dying to plan her daughter's wedding. "Maybe next week, Mom."

Her mother gave her a skeptical look and then disappeared back into her office.

Annoyed by her mother's judgement, Hanna moved to the sink and waved a hand. Immediately the water turned on, filling the basin. After it was three-quarter's full, she placed the dirty dishes in the sink and waved her hand again, causing the water to churn. The spell was an old one that Hanna had perfected years ago. Within ten minutes, the dishes would be sparkling clean, and Hanna could spend her time doing something more useful, like prepping the batter for the next morning's cookies. She'd just added the butter to the large mixer when the bell on the front door chimed.

"Be with you in a minute," Hanna called over her shoulder.

"Take your time, love." His familiar rough voice made gooseflesh pop out on her arms and she scowled.

She hated that Rhys Silver had that effect on her. Why

couldn't she just get over him already? Oh, right. It probably had something to do with the fact that he took care to come in every Friday afternoon during their slow period so that he could flirt with her when no one else was around.

"What do you want, Rhys?" she asked and winced when she heard her exasperated tone. The only thing worse than him causing a physical reaction was letting him know that he got under her skin.

"I was hoping for a large coffee, one of those chocolate scones, and a date for dinner." He said it so casually she actually thought she'd heard him wrong.

She spun, trying to look anywhere but right at him. But he was right there at the counter, taking up all the space with his broad shoulders, thick dark hair, and smiling dark eyes. Rhys had two moods. He was either full of laughter and amusement, or he was brooding and distant. His recent Friday afternoon visits had, without fail, been the former. And it pissed her off because it made dodging him that much harder. "I'm sorry, what was that?"

"Large black coffee, a chocolate scone, and dinner tonight at seven at Woodlines," he said, his lips forming a sexy little half smile that he knew she had trouble resisting.

"Coffee and scone coming right up." Hanna turned and blew out a breath. This was the third week in a row he'd asked her out. And it was going to be the third week in a row she turned him down.

"I hear Woodlines has crab-stuffed trout as the special tonight," he said.

Her mouth started to water with the suggestion.

"Tuna tartare, too, and lobster bisque."

He was speaking Hanna's language, but still, falling back into the friendship he'd blown off a year ago wasn't in her master plan. "Sorry," she said. "I'm busy."

"Really?" He raised both eyebrows, clearly skeptical. "I just ran into Faith on the way in here. She said she was feeling bad because she had to cancel girls' night. Come on, Hanna. I know you're still angry with me. Let me make it up to you."

Dammit, Faith, Hanna thought. It was infinitely easier to dodge him when she legitimately already had plans. That was the danger of living in a small town. Everyone knew everything about everyone. "I just don't think—"

"Hanna!" Mary Pelsh called as she rushed out of her office again. "I've got great news."

"What is it, Mom?" Hanna asked, grateful for the distraction.

"Barb Garber's stepson, Chad, arrived last week. You remember him, don't you? He spent a summer in Keating Hollow and helped us here in the café."

Hanna had a vague recollection of a pale, skinny boy with acne and unruly curly hair that was always hiding his eyes. "Sure, Mom. He was here spending time with his dad and was hoping to get into some performing arts school, right?"

"That's correct. He ended up studying music at a school down in San Francisco." She grinned at her daughter. "He's quite the accomplished pianist now. Anyway, he's moved to Keating Hollow, and I told Barb you'd be happy to introduce him to the locals, grab some dinner, help him get reacquainted. Is seven okay? He could pick you up here, and you won't have to spend another Friday night home alone."

"I don't spend my Friday nights alone," Hanna huffed. "Are you forgetting about Bandit?"

"Bandit is your neighbor's dog, honey," Mary said, rolling her eyes. "That's not even close to the same as male companionship."

Hanna shrugged. "I like hanging out with her. Someone has to when Chelsea works double shifts at the hospital."

"So, can I tell Barb you're good to go?" Mary said, bulldozing over Hanna's dodge.

Silence hung in the air as Hanna tried to swallow her irritation. Not only did she have zero desire to show the new guy around town, her mother had just confirmed to Rhys that she actually didn't have plans that evening. He'd already figured it out, but she'd been planning to make up something about having already texted Noel, Faith's sister. If she still went with that excuse, she'd be lying to her mother as well as Rhys, and the thought made her stomach churn. She never lied to her mom. The woman could always tell anyway. That particular ability was really annoying, but it had conditioned Hanna to always tell the truth.

Rhys cleared his throat.

"Oh, hello Rhys," Mary said, smoothing her black curls as she smiled at him. "Forgive me for being so rude. I didn't even realize you were standing there." She let out a nervous chuckle. "Gosh, I guess I was just a little excited to set Hanna up on a date. It's been a really long time since she—"

"Mom!" Hanna barked.

"What, honey?" Mary blinked innocently at her. "I was just trying to help."

Hanna narrowed her eyes at her mother, trying to figure out her game. Mary Pelsh was not clueless. In fact, Hanna was fairly certain her mother knew that she'd had a thing for Rhys for years. So it didn't make sense for her to try to embarrass her in front of Rhys unless—

"Hanna already has plans tonight," Rhys said. "I'm taking her to dinner at Woodlines and then a late movie over in Eureka. Maybe she can catch up some other time with... what's his name? Chad?"

Mary nodded and beamed as she said, "Yes. Chad. He's

really good looking, too." She leaned into Hanna. "A real frog-to-prince story."

"Right," Rhys said. "Anyway, maybe Hanna can catch up with him another night."

"Oh, well, isn't that lovely," Mary said with a pleased smile. She turned and patted her daughter on the shoulder. "I'll just let Barb know tonight's not a good night. I'm sure Chad will be just fine."

After her mother disappeared back into her office, Hanna eyed Rhys. "I never agreed to dinner."

"You can still back out," he said, shrugging one shoulder. "But then you'll have to hang out with *Chad*." There was a gleam in his eye, one that said he knew exactly what she was going to do. And it both infuriated and amused her. She hated that he knew her so well. It made it impossible to keep him at arm's length.

"Fine. Woodlines at seven. But no movie," Hanna said. "I've been up since five a.m."

His grin widened. "Seven it is."

CHAPTER 2

*R*hys walked into the Keating Hollow brewery feeling like a huge weight had been lifted off his chest. For weeks he'd been trying to break through the walls Hanna had built after Noel and Drew's wedding more than three months ago. He'd been trying to apologize. He'd wanted to get their friendship back on track, but she wasn't having any of it.

Then she'd kissed him.

He'd gotten lost in that kiss and had almost forgotten why they were always going to be better as friends. Damn, he'd wanted to throw caution to the wind, take her home with him, and love her until the sun came up.

Instead, she'd ended the kiss and walked off, her head held high, making him desperate for more. He knew that had been her intention. Hell, he admired her for it. Hanna was full of confidence and fire, the two reasons he'd fallen for her over a decade ago.

But circumstances had killed the dream that they could be a

couple. The best he could hope for was her friendship. He just prayed he could convince her to give him another chance to prove that he wouldn't shut her out of his life, no matter what was going on.

"Hey," Clay Garrison called from behind the bar. "Got a couple hours? We could use an extra pair of hands."

Rhys glanced around the pub. He'd been so preoccupied with his thoughts of Hanna that he hadn't even noticed that every table was full and Sadie, the pub's regular waitress, was darting around with her hair on fire. "Sure, man. But I need to leave by six. I have plans."

"I'll take whatever I can get," Clay said as he slipped out from behind the bar to help Sadie with the tables.

Rhys grabbed an apron, quickly washed his hands, and took over the bar. It didn't take long for him to figure out the crowd had everything to do with a book signing Yvette Townsend was hosting over the weekend. Apparently twenty paranormal romance authors were in town. And hundreds of their fans would be arriving the next day. Since the pub was the Townsend family business, it was the first place Yvette had recommended when the authors asked for dinner recommendations.

"Hey there, Rhys. You're looking extra handsome tonight." The woman who'd just climbed up on a barstool had dark curly hair that was piled up on top of her head, her curls resembling a softer version of medusa. She'd completed her witchy look with a dark violet, lacey dress that cinched at her waist.

"Good evening," he said with his customer service smile. "Have we met?" She seemed familiar, but he couldn't quite place her.

"Sure. I was here about a year ago when I did a book

signing at Yvette's magical bookstore." She held her hand out. "Miranda Moon."

"Right. I remember now." He grabbed her hand and shook before going back to pouring beer from the taps. "Welcome back to Keating Hollow."

The woman glanced down at her hand and frowned.

"Something wrong?" Rhys handed a tray of drinks to Clay and quickly started filling another order.

"Maybe." She peered at him, her expression thoughtful.

He glanced at the beer she'd set in front of her when she sat down. "Is the beer not to your liking? I can get you something else."

"Huh?" Her gaze landed on her drink and she shook her head. "Oh, no. It's fine. Thank you though." She tilted her head to look up at him again and frowned. "Have you been feeling all right? I get the impression that your energy levels might not be one hundred percent. Like maybe you're coming down with a cold."

Rhys stiffened. "What makes you say that?"

She gave him an apologetic shrug. "Sorry. I didn't mean to invade your privacy. I was a healer before I decided to try my hand at writing. It sort of sneaks up on me. Your energy feels a little low. You might want to go see a healer. See if you just need some supplements or something."

"Right. I'll do that," Rhys mumbled.

"I'm sure it's nothing," Miranda said and gave him a bright smile.

"You're probably right," he agreed, having no intention of seeing a healer. Her assessment wasn't a surprise to him. He'd been pushing himself pretty hard lately. *Work hard, play hard* had become his personal mantra over the last few years. He made a mental note to go to Charming Herbs and get the ingredients for a basic energy potion.

"Thanks for the conversation, handsome." Miranda winked at him. "I hope you come by the signing tomorrow. Yvette's having it catered by the Incantation Café. Those scones they make are to die for."

"Maybe." It was a lie. The only way he'd show up was if they ordered food from the brewery or Hanna needed help with a delivery. It just wasn't his idea of fun to stand in line all day with hundreds of other people. Besides, his ereader was already full. Books weren't something he was short on.

"Come on, Rhys," she coaxed. "Give us girls a hero to look at for an hour or so."

He chuckled. "Maybe Jacob will be there. Let him bask in the attention."

"Hmm. I think that sounds like a job for Brian. I met him earlier today. Talk about a flirt." She jerked her head toward the other end of the bar where the man in question was feasting on a basket of wings. "Gotta go recruiting. Have a nice evening, Rhys."

He watched her go and felt that weight he always carried with him return in full force.

～

AT A QUARTER TO SEVEN, Rhys walked into the Incantation Café. The moment he saw Hanna, a smile pulled at the corners of his lips. She was always pretty, but tonight she'd dressed to no doubt torture him. He both loved it and dreaded it. It would take an act of god to not put his hands on her.

Her bronze skin practically glowed against the shimmering gold sweater dress that showed off all her curves. And if that wasn't enough, she was wearing lace-up, knee-high, high-heeled boots that made her legs go on for days.

"Good evening, Rhys," she said, giving him a knowing look.

12

She knew exactly what she was doing to him, and he didn't even care. No man on the planet could be unaffected by her beauty.

He swallowed hard and raised his gaze to her eyes. "You look lovely, Hanna."

"Thanks." She walked past him, her shoulder barely brushing up against his. A small shudder rolled through him, causing his hands to ache to touch her.

Cool it, Rhys, he told himself. Friends. That's what they had been since they were kids, and that's what they were going to continue to be. They had to. He missed her too much. Ever since they'd dated briefly the year before, their relationship had been strained. He knew it was his fault. He'd had a moment of weakness when he asked her out on a real date. And other one when he'd kissed her for the first time. Their relationship had been so easy, so perfect, and it had scared him to death. He'd suddenly known if he let it go any further, there'd be no going back. He'd never be able to let her go, and in the end he'd just hurt her. And that was the one thing he couldn't live with.

Friends. That's what we are and that's what we always will be, he told himself again.

"Are you coming?" she asked from the doorway.

"Rhys! Don't you look nice," Mary Pelsh said from behind him.

He turned and smiled at her. "Thank you, Mrs. Pelsh. So do you."

Hanna's mother rolled her eyes. "Please. I've been here for ten hours and probably have flour in my hair. But you're sweet to say so. You kids go out. Have fun. And Hanna, don't forget to bring me a piece of that lovely tiramisu."

"You got it, Mom," Hanna said cheerily. "Come on, Rhys.

Let's go before I feel too guilty for leaving her here by herself to finish the baking prep."

"Pshh," Mary said, waving her hand. "I wouldn't let you if you tried."

Rhys had no doubt that was true. Mary Pelsh had never made it a secret that she wished the two of them would get together. She'd probably grill Hanna about their evening later.

Hanna slipped her arm through Rhys's and gave him one of her dazzling smiles. "I hope your credit card isn't maxed out, because I'm about to order half of everything on the menu."

"Don't worry, Muffin," he said with a grin. "I came prepared. I haven't forgotten your impressive eating skills."

"You know I hate it when you call me that," she said with mock annoyance. He'd started using the sugary sweet nickname when they were teenagers after she'd put him and four other people to shame in a muffin eating contest.

"No, you don't. Otherwise your lips wouldn't turn up into that tiny little smile every time I say it." He slid his hand down to the small of her back and then adjusted his grip, cupping it around her slender waist, letting himself enjoy the feel of her for just a moment.

She paused and gazed at him, her expression soft. "Be careful, Rhys. With the flirting and the way you're looking at me, a girl could get the wrong impression."

He knew he should drop his hand and take a step back. But he just couldn't. She felt too good. And she wasn't getting the wrong impression. Far from it. He wanted her. Wanted her so badly he could taste it. It was just... under the circumstances... He gave himself a tiny shake and finally did take a step back while shoving his hands into his pockets. Then he gave her a teasing smile. "It's a good thing you wore a stretchy dress. There are six desserts on the menu, and I intend to order at least four."

Her lips twitched, and she shook her head. "Don't wimp out on me now, Silver. Better order all six. That way you'll be sure to get at least one."

"That's my girl," he said with a wink. "I knew I could count on you."

CHAPTER 3

*H*anna savored the crisp citrus flavor of her Sauvignon Blanc as she admired Rhys over the rim of her wine glass. Had he been working out? He was wearing a long-sleeved, button-down shirt, but the sleeves had been rolled up to just below his elbows. And those forearms... holy hell. Her fingers ached to reach out and touch him.

Stop it, Hanna, she told herself. They were just friends. And other than the flirting she'd called him on when he'd picked her up at the café, he was certainly driving solidly in the friend lane.

"I think you should give that guy a try," Rhys said. "What did your mom say his name was?"

"Chad," Hanna said, narrowing her eyes at him. "I thought you stepped in to save me from having to go on a blind date with him. Why are you pushing this now?"

He chuckled softly. "I saw an opening to get you out to dinner with me, and I took it. Our fight has gone on for too long. But that doesn't mean you shouldn't consider this Chad guy. Sounds like he's really talented. Maybe he can teach you scales or something."

Hanna made a face. "You do remember the clarinet fiasco, right? How my teacher told my parents that no matter what keys I used, the 'music' sound like a donkey in heat?"

"You just needed more time to practice. That old bag was expecting too much too fast," he said and took a sip of his own wine.

"I'd been having weekly lessons for two years."

Rhys laughed and then promptly choked on his wine. His eyes were watering by the time he got himself under control, but he grinned at her. "Okay, so music isn't your strong point. But maybe he'll write you a symphony."

Hanna rolled her eyes. "Would you drop it already? I'm not interested in a blind date."

"If you say so."

There was an awkward silence as Hanna wondered why he was so keen on setting her up with the new guy. She assumed it was because he felt guilty that their stint at actual dating hadn't lasted more than a few months. If she was paired off, he wouldn't have to worry about her pining for him. The idea that he might feel sorry for her made her want to hit him, and she scowled.

"Hey," he said softly. "It was just an idea. You don't have to date the piano man. Obviously, you're smart and gorgeous. You can have anyone you want."

Except you, she thought, and then she shook her head as if to dislodge the words from her mind.

"Yes, you can," he said, misinterpreting her thoughts. "Damn, Hanna. You're a model for god's sake."

"An amateur one," she clarified. "It's not like I do regular modeling work."

"You could." He sat back, holding his wine glass, and eyed

her. "I bet if you took off for New York or Los Angeles, you'd be signed to an agency in no time."

Her insides warmed. She knew he wasn't just trying to flatter her. He'd said the same thing many times before. Perhaps it really was time to let go of the fact that she wanted to be his other half. It was obvious he didn't feel the same, and it was time to accept that he loved her, but not in a romantic way.

It was in that moment that she finally admitted to herself just how much she'd missed his friendship. It was time to get over the idea that they might ever be a couple and just accept what he was able to offer. She could do this. If she could just stop staring at his muscular forearms.

"Thanks," she finally said. "But you know I'm not interested in leaving Keating Hollow. I love working at the café. Did I tell you my mom made me a partner?"

He leaned forward, his eyes lighting up at her news. "Really? When did that happen?"

"About six months ago. We've expanded by supplying bakery items to Faith's spa and Yvette's bookstore. Add in the tourists their two businesses bring to this town, and we're suddenly a lot busier than we used to be. I manage the bakery side while Mom manages the rest of the café."

"Wow. That's great, Han." He reached across the table and squeezed her hand. "It's what you always said you wanted."

Hanna beamed. "It is. I wasn't sure the café was going to be big enough to support two households, but we're there. I even moved into my own place a few months ago."

"Really?" His eyes widened in surprise, and then he frowned. "You didn't tell me that."

Was that hurt she saw in his expression? She leaned in, and this time she was the one to grab his hand. "Listen, Rhys. This last year or so… we just weren't close. And I—"

"I know that's my fault," he said stiffly.

She let go of his hand and sat back in her chair. It was true that it was mostly his fault, but since January, she'd been the one giving him the cold shoulder. Now she was ready to put the past behind them. Rhys was her oldest friend. They'd been best friends in high school and when her sister died, he'd been there, holding her up, keeping her going, and giving her a reason to live, not just survive. She cherished him for it. She loved him for it. And letting their failed romantic relationship get in the way of their friendship was stupid. "Let's not play the blame game, okay? I just want my friend back."

"I'm right here, Muffin," he said with a hint of a relieved smile. "Always right here for you."

"Good."

The waitress chose that moment to arrive and take their dessert orders.

"One of everything," Rhys said, handing her the menus. "And coffee for both of us."

"Regular or decaf?" she asked.

"Regular," both Rhys and Hanna said at the same time. As she nodded and walked away, they both laughed. Some things never changed.

"So…" Hanna leaned forward. "I told you my news. What have you been up to? Anything exciting? How's the job at the brewery? Is Clay letting you do any test batches?"

Rhys put down his wineglass. "Actually, yes. Sort of anyway. With Lincoln still recovering from his cancer treatments and the extra-busy tourist season, we've really had to be on our toes." Lincoln Townsend, a pillar in the community, owned the Townsend Brewery and was dealing with a cancer diagnosis. It hadn't been easy for him, but he'd handed the Master Brewer reins over to Clay Garrison so he could concentrate on getting well.

It made sense. Clay was an earth witch and had a talent for such things. Rhys was a water witch, and while that came in handy sometimes, it wasn't the same as being able to manipulate the grains and ingredients that went in the beer batches to make them unique. Still, Rhys had always had an interest in the chemistry of brewing and wanted to try his hand at what could be done without ingredient manipulation.

"What does 'sort of' mean?" Hanna asked.

"It's not beer. It's cider. Lin decided it was time to diversify and wants us to see what we can do with some of those apples in his orchard. Clay's asked me to spearhead the project. If I can come up with something great-tasting, there's potential for me to oversee that arm."

"Rhys!" Hanna cried. "That's incredible. Wow. Have you had any luck yet? Anything worth writing home about?"

He shrugged as if it wasn't any big deal. "I've been experimenting with a few small homebrew batches, just to see what I think of the combinations. We can't really do anything big at the brewery until fall when Lin's apples are ready to harvest. For now, I'm just using fresh-pressed juice."

Hanna pursed her lips and eyed him knowingly. "Just a few experiments? I bet you have dozens of samples already." That's how he was when he was excited about a project. He went all-in until he was satisfied with the results.

He threw his head back and laughed. "You know me entirely too well, Hanna. Yes. I have about three dozen batches. Nothing great yet, though, so don't pester me to taste anything yet."

It was her turn to laugh. He knew her well, too. She was dying to taste-test his first tries. She wanted a reference for when he unveiled a winning brew. "Oh, come on. Not even for your oldest friend?"

He relented immediately, and she was a little surprised. "All right. You can come over on Sunday, but it has to be in the afternoon. I have a thing in the morning."

"Thing?" She raised one eyebrow. "Since when do you get up early on a Sunday?"

"Since I took up hang gliding. It's incredible. The route is out over the Pacific and then we land back on the beach. I swear, it's the best adrenaline rush ever."

"Hang gliding? Seriously?" Excitement shot through Hanna, and she nearly jumped right out of her chair. "I'm coming with you. Oh, my gods, I've always wanted to do that."

But instead of being happy that his friend wanted to join him, Rhys was frowning.

"What?" she asked him, confused. "What's wrong? Are you meeting with someone else and don't want me in the way?"

"No, of course not," he said, shaking his head. His forehead was wrinkled and his eyebrows drawn together when he added, "You can't go hang gliding, Hanna. It's far too dangerous."

"No, it isn't. You go, don't you?" she said, annoyed that he sounded like one of her parents.

"That's different," he said, frowning. "I'm experienced. I've been doing this type of thing for over two years while you've been learning to bake scones and fancy cupcakes. Hang gliding is for someone a little more... athletic."

"I work out!" Then Hanna let out a derisive snort. "Chauvinist much? What, you think I can't learn?"

"That's not... it doesn't have anything to do with the fact that you're a girl. It really is dangerous."

"If you can do it, I can too," she insisted, acutely aware that she was digging in only because he was telling her she shouldn't. Hanna didn't like it when people tried to tell her what to do. She especially didn't like it when that person was Rhys, who thought he was entitled to some kind of say-so over her life even when he'd kept her at arm's length for an entire year.

"Hanna." He pressed his fingertips to his temple. "No. It's just too dangerous. I won't let you."

"Thanks for the vote of confidence." She raised one eyebrow and peered at him. "What are you gonna do? Tell your guy to not take me?"

"Yes, if that's what it takes." There was fire in his gaze as he said the words, and she had no doubt that he would make good on his promise.

"You're something else, you know that?" She placed her elbows on the table and leaned forward. "Do you really think it doesn't worry me when you go rock climbing or skydiving or surfing in the dead of winter?"

"How did you know about the climbing and skydiving?" he asked, eyeing her with suspicion as if he just realized she'd been stalking him. But as much as she'd have wanted to, that wasn't her style and he should know that about her.

She waved an impatient hand. "It's a small community, Rhys. People talk."

His frown deepened as if he couldn't possibly understand why anyone would talk about his extreme sports.

The waitress arrived. She was all smiles as she placed one plate after another on the table. "You two must really love your sweets." After leaving them extra forks and spoons, she quickly returned with the coffee pot and filled their cups. "Anything else I can get for you? Extra cream or sugar?"

"No," they both said. Then Rhys glanced up at her. "Thank you."

Hanna added, "Can you bring us some to go boxes and the check? It looks like I'm going to have to leave sooner than expected."

"Sure."

As soon as she left, Rhys placed his hand over Hanna's. "I'm sorry. I didn't mean to upset you. I just... I worry."

She pulled her hand from his, hating how much she liked his touch. "It's not your job to worry about me, Rhys. I can handle myself."

There was an awkward silence until the waitress brought the to-go boxes. The desserts remained untouched, despite their earlier banter about trying them all. Their server was quick and efficient, helping Hanna get them all boxed up. Then she ran Rhys's credit card and brought Hanna a bag for her boxes.

"Let's go. I have to get up early," Hanna said, standing.

"Han," Rhys said with a sigh. "I was hoping we could take a walk down by the river, like old times."

"Not tonight," she said, grabbing the to-go bag. "Maybe another time."

But when he pressed her on when they could get together again, she dodged. He was doing it again. Trying to keep her "safe." When he'd called off their dating, he'd said it was to protect her. Now she wasn't even allowed to take a hang gliding class because apparently he deemed his own activity too dangerous for her. When had he decided she was made of glass?

"Sure, Hanna. Anything you say." He walked her to his Jeep Wrangler and let her direct him to her new place. Once they were parked at her curb, he turned to her. "Thanks for joining me for dinner. Do I get any of those desserts?"

She shook her head. "Wouldn't want you to gain any weight. You don't want to be out of shape the next time you glide over the ocean, do you? I hear it's really dangerous." She smirked at him and hopped out before he could say anything.

And even though she felt like a total bitch for the way she was acting, she kept her head held high until she disappeared into her small cottage. It wasn't his job to tell her what she should and shouldn't be doing. In fact, she marched right over to her little desk and flipped on her computer. It was time to get a little extreme. Five minutes later, she picked up the phone and tapped Faith's name.

"Hey, Hanna. How was the date?" Faith asked as soon as she picked up the phone.

"It wasn't a date. Are you still free Sunday morning?" They'd talked about getting together for brunch. It was Faith's day off.

"Sure. Wanna go into Eureka and try that new breakfast place? I heard they have biscuits and gravy that is to die for."

"Sure. But first we're going to make a stop at Redwood Coast Adventures."

There was silence on the other end of the line. Then Faith suddenly squealed. "You're ready? Are you sure? You know I've wanted to do this for forever. Talk about a stress reliever. Oh, Em. Gee. Are you sure?"

"I'm sure. I'll pick you up at seven."

CHAPTER 4

*R*hys's footsteps pounded on the dirt path as he finished the last fifty feet of his daily run. Every morning, he rolled out of bed, threw his running shoes on, and took off through the forest behind his small three-bedroom house that sat at the edge of the redwoods. Most days he ran five miles. But that morning, he'd been lost in thought, mostly about Hanna and the way he'd really effed up their date, and ended up logging seven.

His body was slick with sweat, and his muscles were fatigued by the time he let himself in the back door. The scent of bacon hit him, and he groaned. That meant only one thing.

"Rhys? Is that you?" his mother called from the kitchen.

He sighed and turned the corner, finding her standing in front of his stove, making a feast that looked like it would feed a family of six. "Morning, Mom. What are you doing here so early?"

"Early?" she said with a snort. "It's past eight already. What does it look like I'm doing? I'm making you breakfast. Now go shower. This will be ready in about ten minutes."

Rhys glanced at the spread and bit back a grimace. A calorie laden breakfast hadn't been on his agenda that morning. Still, she was his mother, and it wasn't as if he was going to throw her out. Without a word, he crossed the kitchen, climbed the stairs, and disappeared into his bathroom.

Fifteen minutes later, Rhys reappeared in jeans and a T-shirt, his hair still wet.

"Coffee's on the table," Millie Silver said.

"Thanks." Rhys paused to kiss her on the cheek and then moved to the fridge to grab the pitcher of filtered water. Once he had a glass, he sat down at the table and took stock of the feast: eggs, bacon, sausage, biscuits, gravy, and homemade hash browns. There wasn't a vegetable or piece a fruit in sight. "Uh, Mom?"

"Yes, dear?" She placed a waffle in front of him and then slipped into the seat next to him at the end of the table.

"Are you expecting company?"

She took a look at her spread and chuckled. "No. Just us. I guess I got carried away. Well, whatever you don't eat, you can have for leftovers the rest of the week."

"Sure." He grabbed the pure maple syrup and drizzled some on the waffle. It had been a very long time since he'd allowed himself to eat in such a manner. He ate clean most of the time. Lots of fish, salads, fruit and lean meats. There was very little dairy in his diet and not much sugar outside of the beer and ciders he sampled at work. Though he'd been willing to make an exception the night before with Hanna and the dessert fest. His food choices weren't because he was worried about his weight. He just wanted to *feel* good. For the last two years, his clean diet had done that for him.

"Eat, eat," his mother encouraged. "You're too thin."

"No, I'm not." He took a bite of the glorious waffle and almost moaned at how good it tasted. But he held back the sound of approval. The last thing he wanted to do was encourage Millie to do this more often. After he swallowed, he glanced at his mother's plate. "Aren't you eating?"

"Yes, but I wanted to wait for you to get your fill first." She smiled sweetly at him, her green eyes dancing with triumph.

"Mother, you're being a little intense. Eat with me, or I'm going to put my fork down."

"Fine. Don't be so testy." She filled her plate with breakfast, but instead of eating, she just stared at him.

Rhys sighed. "Just say it."

"Say what?" she asked innocently.

"Whatever it is you're dying to say." He took a sip of his coffee.

"Oh, fine." She flipped her dark hair over her shoulder and leaned in, her round face eager and full of excitement. "How was your date with Hanna? Are you two getting back together?"

He'd known that was what she wanted to talk about and wondered if the carb fest was an attempt at putting him into a food coma so that his defenses would be down. "It wasn't a date."

"Please. Was I born yesterday? You took her to dinner. You paid. You took her home. What else could it be?"

He blinked at his mother. She'd pulled back and had her hand resting on her slightly pudgy middle, giving him that look that said she wasn't taking any of his crap. "How did you know I paid or that I took her home?"

"I have my sources," she said primly but then shook her head. "Never mind that. Are you going to tell me what's going on with Hanna, or am I going to have to ask her?"

Oh, hell, he thought. She would march right into the Incantation Café and do just that. Millie Silver and Mary Pelsh had been friends since they were both kids. The Silvers and

Pelshes were like extended family already. He had no trouble imagining Hanna sitting down and telling his mother that he'd implied she was too weak to join him on a hang gliding adventure. And not only would Millie be angry he'd acted like a Neanderthal, she wouldn't like his choice of activity either. "We had dinner. It was fine. Then I took her home."

"That's it?" Millie asked incredulously. "That's all I get? 'It was fine?'"

He chuckled. "What were you expecting? To find her here this morning? Is that why you made a feast?"

Millie's face flushed, and she glanced away.

"You did! That's exactly what you thought would happen. Geez, Mother. What if she was here? Weren't you afraid you'd embarrass her? Or me for that matter?"

"I'm sure Hanna would've been happy to see me," she said, holding her head high now.

"Sure, Mom." He shook his head and dug into the rest of his waffle. And then just to make her happy, he ate a few pieces of bacon. "Okay, that's all I can do right now."

Millie looked at all of the food still on the table and blew out a breath. "I really did get carried away, didn't I?"

"A little." Rhys winked at her and started to clear the table.

As they stored the leftover food in plastic containers, his mother asked, "Rhys?"

"Yeah?"

"Why did you break up with Hanna last year?"

He froze. She'd managed to keep from asking him that after he'd ended it. After so much time, he thought he'd managed to dodge the question.

"Well?" she prompted.

"You know why, Mom." He turned away from her and stacked the plastic containers in his fridge.

She placed a hand on his arm and very gently said, "You aren't your father. Or your grandfather for that matter."

He was still as he stared unseeingly into the fridge.

"It's not fair to either of you to keep her at arm's length because you're afraid of what might happen."

Her words cut him straight to the bone, and the pain seared right through his chest, making it hard to breathe. He pictured Hanna in a gorgeous white wedding dress, standing next to him down by the river. She'd have red flowers in her dark curly hair, and he'd be in a tux. Then the image shifted, and they were holding hands at the beach, their beautiful golden child laughing and running toward the ocean's edge. Longing filled him, making him ache for her. He could think of nothing that would make him happier than having her by his side for the rest of his days.

Then he saw his father's lifeless body lying on his mother's kitchen floor and he shook himself. "No. I can't do that to her. I won't."

"Rhys you have to stop—"

"That's enough," he said with quiet authority. "I've made my decision. Nothing you can say will change it."

"If that's really how you feel..." she said, sounding defeated.

"It's really how I feel," he agreed and then gently took the dish she was holding out of her hand. "Thank you for breakfast. Go relax. I'll clean up."

She hesitated, but when he gently nudged her, she relented. "All right. I just want you to be happy, Rhys. You know that, right?"

"I do." He gave her a one-armed hug. "I think next time you want to make sure I'm happy, a salmon omelet will do instead of the all-you-can-eat buffet."

"Now that sounds lovely. Maybe with bagels and lox, too."

He laughed. "Go relax. I'll finish up in here and then we can head to town. I know you want to hit that book signing."

"You're taking me to the signing?" she asked, her eyes lighting up.

"Sure. I'll drop you off, and you can meet me at the brewery when you're done. I'm sure Clay could use the help."

"You're a good boy." She patted his arm again and then disappeared into his living room. A second later, he heard his television come on and the sound of some cable news talk show.

He stood at his sink and rubbed at the ache in his chest. Damn. His mother had completely knocked him off his axis. Again. Maybe it was because he'd spent the evening with Hanna the night before and had a great time right up until he'd been an ass. Or maybe it was because his mom pressed buttons he didn't let anyone else touch.

It didn't matter. Nothing had changed. Rhys knew what it was like for his mother when his dad had died. He also knew what it was like to grow up without a father. And since Rhys carried the gene that caused his father's and grandfather's early deaths, marriage and a family wasn't in the cards for him... no matter how much he loved Hanna.

CHAPTER 5

*T*he best thing about being busy was that Hanna didn't have time to dwell on her nonexistent love life. It was just as well that her date with Rhys had ended prematurely, because five o'clock came awfully early. She'd rolled into the café a half hour later and spent the next few hours baking the treats for the book signing. By the time the clock struck noon, she had more cookies, cupcakes, and scones than she knew what to do with.

She poked her head out into the café and grimaced. The line was out the door still, which meant no one had a spare moment to help her carry the large pink boxes down to Hollow Books.

"Oh, gosh, Hanna. I'm sorry," Candy, her cousin, said from her spot at the register. "Can you wait about ten minutes and see if we can knock this line down?"

"No, it's okay. I've got it." Hanna started stacking the boxes on the counter. "I'll just have to make a couple of trips. It'll be fine."

"Chad can help you, dear," Barb Garber said.

Hanna glanced over at the woman. She was standing near the pickup counter, gesturing to a tall blond guy who looked an awful lot like the actor who played Eric on *True Blood*. Hanna's gaze traveled over his long lean frame and lingered on his chiseled face. Whoa. That was *Chad*?

"Hello." He walked over to the counter and picked up all six of her boxes with ease. "Need these hauled out to a car?"

"Um, no." She shook her head, trying to get control of her tongue. Geez, that man was gorgeous. "They need to go down to Hollow Books. I was just going to walk."

"I'll do it if you show me the way." His muscles flexed, and she thought she might swoon.

"Thank you!" Candy called to him as she rushed to make another latte.

"Right. Thank you," Hanna echoed. "Let me just grab the last two." She ran into the back, collected the rest of the boxes, and hurried out into the lobby. "This way."

Chad followed her out of the café and fell into step beside her out on the cobbled sidewalk.

"This is really nice of you," Hanna said, finally finding her voice. "I know your mom sort of just threw you to the wolves back there. It's hard to refuse when a bunch of townies are watching you."

He chuckled. "It's fine. Really. Maybe this way she'll stop asking if I've called that nice girl at the café yet." He grinned at her. "I think our moms are working the setup pretty hard."

It was Hanna's turn to laugh. "Yes, they appear to be a little focused on setting us up, don't they?"

He gave a slight shrug. "I think it's a worthy cause."

"You do, huh?" A warm little flutter tickled her abdomen. "Are you angling for a dinner date, Chad Garber?"

"With a pretty girl like you? Absolutely. Just name a date and time and I'll be there."

All of the stress and frustration that had plagued Hanna since the night before fled, and she suddenly found herself grinning at the man. "Any time, huh? How about tomorrow night? We could try the Cozy Café."

"Perfect," he said with a nod. "Tomorrow night it is. Six?"

"Works for me." Hanna was so busy smiling up at him she completely missed the entrance of Hollow Books and only stopped when she was just about to run into the massive line of readers lined up to get in. "Oops!" She turned around. "The front door is back there."

"Ah, I wondered if this was the place. Nice window display," he said.

Hanna peered into the window and gasped. Jacob and Yvette had outdone themselves this time. There was a large picture frame with a hologram portrait of one of the signing authors holding her book open along with a feathered quill that scribbled her signature. The author gave an exaggerated wink, and then the author's image changed to another one and the quill did its thing again. Hanna had a feeling that if they stood there long enough, the author portraits would rotate through each of the signing authors for the event.

"They are something else," Hanna said, shaking her head.

The door popped open, and Yvette poked her head out and motioned for them to get inside. The chestnut-haired beauty was bubbling with excitement for her big day. "Stop gawking. We have goodies to put on display."

"The window is amazing, Vette," Hanna said. "I swear, I need you and Jacob to do something for the café. We're the only one on the block that doesn't have something great for the tourists to drool over."

"You have the cupcakes. They are plenty drool-worthy," Yvette said, leading them across the store to the coffee bar. She unloaded the bakery boxes from Chad's arms and then stood back and appraised him. "Well, now. Who is this handsome fellow?"

He held his hand out. "Chad Garber. I just moved to Keating Hollow last week."

"And you've already latched onto Hanna? Smart man." Yvette shook his hand and gave him a conspiratorial wink. "She's gorgeous, right?"

Hanna gave Yvette a warning glare, but Yvette just grinned at her.

"She definitely is," Chad agreed. "And lucky me, she agreed to go to dinner with me tomorrow night."

"She did, did she?" Yvette gave him another appraising glance. "Smart man. You don't waste any time, do you?"

"Stop!" Hanna threw her hands up in the air. "I'm standing right here."

"We know," Yvette said with a laugh.

Rolling her eyes, Hanna slipped behind the coffee counter and went to work plating and arranging the pastries for their event.

"You don't have to do that," Yvette said. "Brinn can handle it."

Hanna glanced across the store and spotted the store's assistant manager running around, fixing book displays and fetching things for the authors who were set up around the store. "Does she have a clone I don't know about?"

Yvette followed Hanna's gaze and winced. "Okay, so she's a little frantic. I better go help." She grabbed Hanna around the shoulders and gave her a quick hug. "Thank you! You're the best."

"I know." Hanna patted her arm and then gave her a little shove. "Now go have the best darn signing that ever existed."

"We plan to." Yvette rushed off to finish the last-minute details before they let the crowd in, leaving Hanna and Chad to the pastries.

Chad, who'd been watching her arrange the cupcakes on a plate, slipped behind the counter and opened the next box. "Want me to do the same with these?"

"You don't have—"

"I know I don't," he said, giving a dismissive wave. "But I'm planning on Keating Hollow being my home for a good while. Being neighborly seems like the best way to meet people."

"You're something else," she said with a small shake of her head. "Okay, handsome. How about you place these little sugar cookies on top of the cupcakes and I'll do the arranging."

He glanced down at the cookies that had been decorated to look just like the bookshop, and his eyes widened. "Did you make these?"

Hanna nodded. "Mom and I finished those yesterday. Aren't they adorable?"

"They're fantastic."

With Chad helping her, they got the desserts unboxed and setup in pretty displays in no time.

"Oh gods, those are gorgeous," Noel Townsend said, stopping in front of the display. "Hanna, you've outdone yourself."

Hanna lifted her shoulders and chin, practically preening with the compliment. "Thanks, Noel. Does Yvette have you working here today?"

"No. We have some authors over at the inn, too. I'm here to steal some of the cupcakes for them." Noel Townsend was one of Yvette's sisters, but the two didn't look anything alike. Noel had honey-blond hair that was swept up into a fancy twist, but she was wearing jeans and a T-shirt. Her only jewelry was the large diamond on her left hand that Drew, her deputy sheriff fiancé, had put there last year.

"Need help? I can carry some for you," Hanna said automatically.

"Nah." Noel put some in one of the discarded bakery boxes. "This is plenty. We're sending the readers over here for the goodies."

"Okay. Well, if there's anything more I can do, just let me know." Hanna clasped her hands together nervously. Only she didn't know why her nerves were jumpy. This wasn't her event, and Yvette was excellent at putting them together. She was sure it was going to be fabulous.

"Hanna, if you want any books signed, do it now," Yvette called from across the room. "I'm getting ready to let them in."

Hanna glanced around the room and nearly gasped when she spotted two of her favorite authors. "I'll be right back," she whispered to Chad. "I see an author or two I need to meet."

"I'll go with you." He slipped his hand down to her elbow, and just like that the pair of them were gliding across the room.

She glanced up at him. "You're awfully smooth, you know that?"

He gave a low chuckle. "I'm just trying to keep the prettiest girl in Keating Hollow in my sight. I don't want to miss out on that lunch I've been planning to invite her to."

"Lunch, really?"

He glanced at his watch. She blinked at him, surprised to see the timepiece on his wrist. No one wore actual watches anymore. No one but Chad Garber, apparently. "Yeah, lunch. It's almost twelve-thirty. How about that brewpub that's here in town? I hear the beer has recently started to win some awards."

It had. Once Clay took over from Lin, he started

experimenting with special seasonal brews, and the latest one to win a blue ribbon was called Epic Red and had notes of pomegranate and citrus. It was Hanna's favorite. The only problem with heading to the pub was that Rhys worked there. But Rhys didn't usually work until Saturday nights, if he worked on Saturdays at all. Lunch should be okay. She glanced up at Chad. "Sure. Sounds good."

"Great. After you get your books signed, we'll head over." He swept his hand out in front of him. "After you."

Hanna hurried to complete her task before Yvette let in the masses and then followed Chad outside. The spring day was warm in the sun, and flowers were blooming everywhere. Someone had spelled the wisteria vines climbing the lampposts to wave at the pedestrians who walked by, making the magical town as cheery as Hanna had ever seen it. "You picked a good time to move here," Hanna said. "Just last month everything was still gray with not much sign of life."

"I bet this town really goes all out at Christmas, though," he said, shoving his hands into his pockets.

"That's very true," Hanna said with a nod. "But I don't want to ruin the surprise."

He groaned. "You're going to make me wait eight months to unlock the secrets of a Keating Hollow Christmas?"

"That's right." A spark of joy had settled in her chest, and Hanna couldn't help but conclude it was a good thing she'd decided to let Chad take her out. She needed some fun in her life. All Rhys wanted to do was wrap her in bubble wrap. And not in the sexy way.

"Hey, are you okay?" Chad asked, giving her a concerned glance.

"Sure. Why?"

"You just looked... I don't know, sad? Upset? That smile

vanished and was replaced by a frown. I just wanted to make sure everything was all right."

"Oh, sorry," she said. "I was just thinking about a friend. We kind of got into a fight last night. It's nothing. I'm sure it will blow over."

"Anything serious?" he asked.

"No. Not really." As much as she hated that she was still fighting with Rhys, this too would blow over, and in a week or so they'd likely go right back to being the buddies they always were.

"That's good. So tell me more about yourself, Hanna. I already know you're a baker. What else makes you, Hanna Pelsh?"

His question was so straightforward that it actually made her chuckle a little. "Well, Chad. I've lived in Keating Hollow my whole life. The only thing I ever really wanted to do career-wise was be a part of the café. I'm happy to say that I'm a full partner, so that worked out. But I also do a little bit of modeling, and I've been known to help out the Townsends at their various businesses when they need an extra pair of hands. And that's about it, really."

He glanced down at her, his blue gaze interested. "So, you're close to your family. I like that. Any siblings, or is it just you and your parents?"

Her heart ached the way it always did when she thought of Charlotte. It had been just over a decade since they'd lost her. The pain had been unbearable for months. Hanna honestly thought that the only way she'd gotten through it was because of Rhys. He'd been there every step of the way, supporting her, lifting her up, giving her strength. She'd never really recovered from the loss, and even now she felt her eyes burn with tears as she let herself remember her sister's vivacious smile. "I had a sister," she said, staring at her feet. "Charlotte.

She passed away from a very rare autoimmune disease that had no cure."

"Damn, Hanna. I'm sorry," he said, taking her hand in his. "I understand how hard that must be. You miss her a lot, don't you?"

Hanna nodded and glanced up to see the sincere expression on his face. "Always."

"Yeah. I miss my mom, too. We lost her about five years ago. Drunk driver hit her on a rainy night."

"Gosh. Taken just like that, no warning," Hanna said in a hushed whisper. She'd stopped right there on the sidewalk to stare up at him. "That's got to be worse. We at least knew Charlotte was sick."

He gave her a small, sad smile. "I don't think we can categorize loss that way. It's hard and human and raw. If we're lucky, the worst it does is leave a hole that hopefully can be masked by a lifetime of love and fond memories."

"Gah." Hanna wiped at her eyes. "Isn't that the truth." She slipped her arm through his and bobbed her head, motioning for them to get moving again. "Tell me your favorite memory of your mother."

Chad let out a chuckle. "My favorite. Hmm. I think that would have to be when I planted a quarter because I wanted to prove her wrong about money not growing on trees. She helped me water the spot for two entire weeks, all the while telling me it was a useless experiment. She was positive that quarter wasn't going to turn into anything. But then..." He grinned down at her. "Two weeks to the day that I planted it, I came home from kindergarten and found a small tree had popped up overnight. Quarters were taped to the leaves."

Hanna blinked up at him. "A tree just appeared while you were at school?"

"Sure," he said with a nod. "She went and bought a small

lemon tree, planted it, and then supplied the quarters. We harvested them that day, but they never grew back, obviously."

"That's really sweet. How long did you go on thinking money grew on trees?"

He laughed. "I guess it was until the lemons started to sprout. A couple of months. But I always secretly hoped the quarters would return. She told me the quarters sprouted because I believed they would. To this day, I figure if I wish hard enough, then money might start growing on lemon trees." He winked at her. "Or maybe it just means I need to move south and start a citrus orchard."

"I think I love your mom," Hanna said.

He nodded. "Everyone did. Now, tell me your favorite memory of your sister."

"Oh, that's easy." Warmth spread through Hanna as she remembered Charlotte placing a daisy corsage on her wrist that cold night in December. "It was my Freshman year in high school, my first formal dance, and my date cancelled at the last minute."

"Tragic," he said with just the right amount of sympathy.

"Very." She paused in front of a Spoonful of Magic and smiled at the window display. Chocolate bells danced around a book display featuring many of the authors participating in the signing. There was a chalkboard note that said if customers produced a signed book, they'd get 10% off. She loved that Miss Maple was working with Yvette to advertise the event.

"So what did your sister do?" Chad asked, prompting her to continue.

"She called my friend Rhys and talked him into taking me." The memory of Rhys, showing up in a suit and holding that daisy corsage, made her eyes mist again. Her date had canceled to take another girl, and she'd been devastated. But then Rhys had been there and spent the evening with his arm wrapped around her and holding her close while they danced. He'd even leaned in and given her a somewhat chaste kiss on the lips when he was certain the jackass was watching. He'd been perfect in every way. Damn him. It was the night she'd fallen for him. "Anyway, he showed up with a corsage that I'm sure Charlotte ordered because it was made of my favorite flowers. And then we went with her and her boyfriend Drew. The worst night of my teenage life turned into one of the best."

"She sounds wonderful. So does your friend Rhys. Are you still friends with him?"

Hanna suppressed a sigh and nodded. "Yeah. We're still friends."

Chad reached out and grabbed her hand, squeezing it slightly. His tone was a little wistful when he added, "There's something special about having friends that you've known for that long."

They continued on toward the pub. "Do you have many friends from your formative years?"

"Yes, but we rarely see each other, and it's been a while since I've been in touch. Our professions require us to move too much. But if I picked up the phone and reached out, they'd be there."

"What kind of profession keeps you on the move? It occurs to me I've spilled my life story, but you've been elusive." She narrowed her eyes at him and gave him a conspiratorial glance. "What is it? Hired hit man?"

He snickered. "Hardly. I'm a professional pianist. I go where the jobs are. Or I did. I'm semi-retired now."

Now that he mentioned it, she did remember her mother saying he was an accomplished pianist. "Retired? But you can't be older than thirty-two, thirty-three at most. Nah. I don't believe it. I'm going with hired hitman."

"Thirty-two," he confirmed. "And while it's true I have been making my living as a pianist, I don't want to spoil your delusions. So we'll just say I'm planning to hide out here and teach piano until the heat backs off."

Hanna laughed. "You're fun."

"So are you."

CHAPTER 6

"*T*hanks, buddy," Clay said, slapping Rhys on the back. "It's good of you to help two days in a row."

"It's no problem," Rhys said with a shrug. "The town is packed today. I figured it'd be a zoo."

"You got that right." Clay pulled the tap on the chocolate stout and tilted the glass to keep the head down. "I think we'll be all right after the lunch rush."

"Whatever you need, man." Rhys moved down the bar, handing a couple of women some menus. After taking their drink orders, he got busy pouring their beers.

It didn't take long for the place to fill up with book lovers, and he was so busy he didn't even notice Hanna had arrived until Clay materialized beside him and asked, "Who's the pretty boy with your girl?"

"My girl?" Rhys's head jerked up and immediately his gaze landed on Hanna. She was as stunning as usual in her jeans and tight T-shirt that hugged her curves. He loved the way her dark curls were pulled back into a wild ponytail, showing off her long neck.

"Who is that dude?" Clay asked, sounding irritated.

"What?" Rhys finally glanced at Hanna's companion and felt his entire body tense. Son of a... He wasn't one to pay much attention to another guy's looks, but hell. The guy grinning at Hanna looked like he belonged on a movie poster. And she was leaning in, laughing, her eyes sparkling the way they did when she was having a good time.

"You better get over there and stake your claim, or else it looks like someone's gonna be invading your territory," Clay said.

"My territory?" Rhys let out a humorless snort. "What are you? A caveman? Besides, Hanna isn't *my* girl."

"Sure, Rhys. You just keep telling yourself that." Clay shook his head. "But when you wake up next month and find that she's officially off the market, you're going to hate yourself for not doing anything about it."

Rhys sucked in a sharp breath at the idea of Hanna with Mr. Hollywood over there.

Clay chuckled. "That's what I thought."

"Excuse me." Rhys slipped out from behind the counter and made his way over to them. Without saying a word, he put the menus on the table.

"Rhys. Uh, hi." Hanna pressed her hand to her throat as she glanced up at him, her mouth in a tight smile. "I thought you weren't working until later."

"The lunch shift needed help. Who's your friend?" He had been trying for friendly, but the question came out more as an unspoken accusation, and he swallowed a groan. That was uncalled for.

Her hand moved to the table, her eyes narrowing in irritation, just as they had the night before when he'd told her hang gliding was too dangerous for her.

Here it comes, he thought. She was going to rip his head off and he'd deserve it. He braced himself for her wrath.

But when she spoke, her annoyed look vanished and her lips curled into a self-satisfied smile. "Rhys, this is Chad Garber. Barb's stepson. You remember my mom mentioning him, right?"

Oh, hell! This Captain America was Chad? The same Chad he'd encouraged Hanna to go out with just the night before? Jesum Crow. He'd brought this fresh hell on himself. "Hello, Chad. Nice to meet you," Rhys said with a short nod of acknowledgment. "Didn't take long to find the prettiest girl in town, did it?"

Chad frowned as he glanced from Rhys to Hanna and back to Rhys. "Hey, man. Am I stepping in the middle of something here?"

Rhys had to give him props for diving into the issue head on, but he sure as hell didn't know how to answer that question.

"No. Of course not," Hanna said. "Like I said earlier, Rhys and I have been friends for a long time. He's just acting like an overprotective big brother." She glanced up at Rhys, glaring at him.

Behaving like a brother was the furthest thing from Rhys's mind, but short of laying his heart out on the table, there wasn't anything he could say to refute her explanation that would make any sort of sense. So he just shrugged and said, "Best friend might be more accurate than brother. Gotta make sure the new guy knows you have people watching out for you."

Hanna rolled her eyes. "Don't listen to him, Chad. I'm perfectly capable of taking care of myself."

"Of course you are," Rhys agreed. "That doesn't mean I

won't want to kick the ass of anyone who doesn't treat you right." He nodded to Chad. "I'm sure you understand."

Chad gave an uncomfortable laugh and said, "You don't have to worry about me. I'm just here for the good beer and conversation."

"Right." Rhys pulled out an order pad. "What can I get you?"

An hour later, after Rhys had paid far too much attention to Hanna and Chad, Hanna finally popped up out of her chair and stalked over to the bar. She stood right in front of Rhys, her hands on her hips. "Can I talk to you for a moment?"

"Uh, sure. What's up?" he asked as if he didn't know she was pissed.

"This way." She jerked her thumb toward the back of the pub and strode off as if she owned the place.

Rhys was amused. Hanna and her sister Charlotte had grown up with the Townsend girls. No one would think twice about her making herself at home in the employees-only section of the brewery. He followed her into the small area they used for testing brew batches and shut the door. "Okay. What did you need? Advice on how to ditch Chad?"

"Are you kidding me right now?" she said, her tone low and full of warning. "What's wrong with you, Rhys Silver? Last night, you told me to go out with this guy. And you've been singing the 'just friends' mantra for months now. You're acting like a jealous boyfriend and honestly, all you're doing is pissing me off."

"I was…" Shit. She was right, of course. He was acting like a jealous boyfriend because he was green with envy that she was out with Chad and not him. It didn't seem to matter that Rhys had been the one that broke things off or was holding her at arm's length. He just wanted her and couldn't seem to make himself stop being an asshole. "I'm sorry, Han. You're right. I guess it's just hard to see you with him." It was the first honest thing he'd said to her in ages. "Can you maybe just not flaunt him in front of me?"

She looked at him in amazement. Then she shook her head and snorted as if she was completely fed up. "You're incredible, you know that?" The statement wasn't a compliment, judging by the sneer she gave him. "First of all, I thought you didn't work until tonight, so I certainly wasn't trying to flaunt my date in front of you. Not that it's a date anyway. He helped me carry some boxes to Yvette's store. I'm buying him lunch as a thank you."

"Oh, I—"

"But secondly, if it was a date, then it's none of your damned business," she added, plowing right over him. "You can't have this both ways, Rhys. You had your shot. In fact, you had about a million of them. You're the one who put the brakes on whatever that was between us last year. And you're the one who keeps telling me we're better as friends. Fine! Friends it is. But you don't get to act like you have any say in who I see. Got it?"

Rhys swallowed and nodded since he didn't trust himself to speak. If he did, he might beg her to show Chad the door and meet him back at his place in a half hour.

"Good." She sucked in a deep breath, visibly trying to calm herself. "Now that we have that settled, I think it's best if we take a break from each other. I need some space."

He hated that idea. The truth was he really missed her. Missed her laugh, her smile, her willingness to call him out on his crap. She was strong and full of fire and the only woman he wanted to spend time with. But the way she was looking at him, her eyes pleading with him to give her a break, there was only one thing he could do. "Sure, Muffin. We can take a break. I'll be here when you're ready to talk again. I'm sorry. I..." He sighed. "Don't take too long, okay?

Who else am I going to get to watch the Hallmark channel with me?"

That got a chuckle out of her. "I bet your mom would be up for it."

He scoffed. "Please. Mom is a *Game of Thrones* type. She'd probably throw her popcorn at the screen."

Hanna reached up and patted his cheek. "Just record them on your DVR. Maybe next month sometime, we can have a marathon."

"Can we turn it into a drinking game? A shot every time a town festival needs to be saved or an almost-kiss is interrupted?"

"Sure," she said, sadness creeping into her dark gaze. "We can do that." Then she turned and walked out.

Rhys followed, but he stood at the bar and watched as Chad stood and wrapped an arm around her shoulders. She leaned into him and let him guide her out of the pub.

So this is what my life is going to be like without her, Rhys thought as he felt the pangs of loss course through his body. *Way to go, dumbass.*

CHAPTER 7

*R*hys hopped out of the shuttle in the parking lot of Redwood Coast Adventures, adrenaline still coursing through his veins. The hang gliding trip had been exhilarating. He loved the freedom and the opportunity to get out of his own head when he was flying through the air, nothing but the wind between him and the earth. Usually the activity left him feeling centered, more in control, as if letting go while up in the air helped him get right with his world. But not this time. Today, all he could think about was Hanna walking arm in arm with *Chad*.

Hanna hadn't done one thing wrong, while Rhys had been an ass. And he hadn't just been rude to Chad, he'd snapped at Clay and Sadie, too. Yesterday hadn't been his best day. He'd apologized to his coworkers, but he hadn't talked to Hanna yet. Chances were, she wasn't interested in hearing from him anyway. Who could blame her? He'd dated her for a few months, called it off, and then proceeded to keep his distance because it was just too damned hard to be around her and be unable to touch her or kiss her or…

Rhys shook his head. That line of thought was getting him nowhere. He needed another fix. Another flight. Another adventure. Something to get Hanna and Chad off his mind. He walked toward the small office, intent on booking another round on the hang glider, when he spotted a familiar RAV4 with a daisy decal on the back of the SUV. His gaze immediately locked on the custom license plate. BAKE4U. There was no mistake. That was Hanna's RAV4.

He glanced around the parking lot, noting a small crowd of people at the nearby food truck. Then the driver of the shuttle called to them, indicating it was time to board. The crowd moved as one and at first, he didn't see her. But then a tall man quickened his pace, revealing Faith Townsend and Hanna, moving quickly toward the bus.

Rhys took off running toward the shuttle, his heart pounding against his ribcage. "Hanna!"

The woman in question paused and glanced around in confusion. Then she spotted him, and a look of complete defiance claimed her pretty face. She waited with her hands on her hips for him to catch up to them.

"Hey," he said, giving her an easy smile and then nodding at Faith. "What are you two doing here?"

"Skydiving," Hanna said, her tone laced with a challenge.

Rhys blinked. "What?"

"Let's go, ladies," the bus driver called. "It's time to get moving."

"You heard me," Hanna said, waving Faith onto the bus. Once her friend stepped inside, Hanna turned to him. "Someone told me hang gliding was too dangerous, so I changed plans."

"But skydiving?" Rhys asked. "You couldn't find anything a little closer to the ground?" The thought of her free falling through the air terrified him. Rationally, he knew Redwood

Coast Adventures had a stellar reputation for safety and if he was going to recommend a skydiving outfit to anyone, it would be RCA. But that didn't mean accidents couldn't happen. There'd been one just last month down in southern California where a shoot didn't open. Panic started to claw at his throat.

"Nope," she said and disappeared onto the bus.

Rhys moved to follow, but the bus driver frown at him. "You're not on my list, Mr. Silver. Did you sign up for this adventure, too?"

He shook his head. "No, but—"

"Sorry. We're all booked. But if you go see Jesse at the reservation counter, I'm sure she can fit you in later today or next weekend."

Rhys looked up into Hazel's friendly eyes and just shook his head. He was there often enough that the entire staff knew him. He could push his luck and probably get a seat on the bus, but he backed off, knowing Hanna wouldn't appreciate his interference. Besides, what good would that do? He could spend the entire bus ride out to the plane trying to talk Hanna out of going, but he'd only make a fool of himself. She wasn't interested in his opinion. She'd made herself abundantly clear. Instead he nodded to the bus driver. "Thanks, Hazel. Have a safe trip."

"Always."

The shuttle door closed, and Rhys stood there in the deserted parking lot, watching the bus disappear down the street. He slowly made his way back to his Jeep, climbed in, and took off without making another reservation to fly. All he could think about was Hanna falling out of the sky. And the next thing he knew, he was pulling his Jeep into another parking lot, the one adjacent to the drop zone used by Redwood Coast Adventures. Rhys killed the engine and waited, ignoring the warning in his mind that he was being unreasonable. He just needed to make sure she was safe, and then he'd go.

The sun shone overhead, and the day was one of those perfect spring days, no fog in sight. If he was being honest with himself, it was the perfect day for a skydiving trip. One couldn't ask for better conditions. That didn't mean his insides weren't jumping around like crazy, though.

The distant whine of the plane sounded overhead, and Rhys glanced up, catching the first jumpers as they hurled through the air. There was no way to know which of the jumpers were Hanna or Faith, so Rhys kept an eye on all of them, holding his breath while the first pack opened up and the chute shot into the air. Three more followed without incident. The last two were still lying flat-out, no chute in sight. Not yet anyway.

"Come on," he said, counting down from ten as a way to calm himself. Ten, nine, eight, seven—" *Whoosh.* One chute deployed. "Six, five, four—" *Whoosh.*

Relief flooded through Rhys, and he sat back in his Jeep, wondering if he should ask his doctor about anxiety meds. What the hell was wrong with him? He'd been skydiving more times than he could count. He'd even considered becoming an instructor at one point. The fact that he was sitting in his Jeep, spying on Faith and Hanna to make sure nothing went wrong with a jump that was statistically safer than the risk of a car accident, was mildly insane.

Shaking his head, he cranked the starter, put the Jeep in reverse, and started to back up. Only when he glanced back at the drop zone, he noticed the wind had picked up and one of the jumpers was struggling to keep their feet under them as they landed. He stepped on the brake and put the Jeep in park just in time to see the jumper lose control and fall face-first into the dirt as the chute dragged them a good ten feet.

The instructor was already running in the person's direction. Rhys pushed his door open and immediately heard Faith Townsend cry, "Hanna! Ohmigod! Are you all right?"

Rhys took off at a dead run. "Hanna!"

Faith turned, and her mouth dropped open into a shocked "O" at his presence, but Rhys only had eyes for the girl who was now sitting up and clutching at her ankle.

"Let's get the gear off of you first, and then we'll check on your leg, okay?" Rob, the instructor, said in a kind and gentle voice. "That gust of wind just came out of nowhere. We're lucky it wasn't worse."

"Hanna?" Rhys dropped down on the other side of her, noting there was a scratch on her face and dirt everywhere. "What's wrong, love?"

She turned to him, her expression pinched with pain. "It's my ankle. I twisted it."

"Just twisted?" Rhys took her hand in his and caressed her thumb, trying to soothe her.

"I don't know."

"Okay. Everything's going to be fine. As soon as they get you free of this gear, I'll get you to the hospital."

Hanna groaned.

"Best to get an x-ray, Han," Faith said.

"Definitely," the instructor said as he slipped Hanna's harness off.

Rhys stood and swept Hanna up into his arms. "I'll take her."

"What about my car?" Hanna asked. "It's back at the office."

"I'll get it and meet you at the hospital," Faith said. "Just give me your keys."

Hanna dug into her pocket and handed the keys to her friend. "Guh. Why am a such a klutz? Everyone else managed to land on their feet just fine."

"It's not your fault, love," Rhys said. "The wind just picked up at the last minute. It happens sometimes."

"He's right," the instructor said. "You were doing great until the wind hit your chute."

"Okay." Hanna leaned into Rhys's chest and closed her eyes. "Can we go? It hurts."

"Sure." He nodded to Rob. "I've got her from here."

"Let me know how it turns out, okay?" Rob asked. "We take injuries seriously around here."

"I know you do," Rhys said. "I'll give you a call." He nodded to Faith. "You don't have to come to the hospital. I can get her home."

Faith shook her head. "No. I'll meet you there."

"Whatever you want, Faith. See you later." He tightened his hold on Hanna and took off to his Jeep at a clipped speed.

CHAPTER 8

*H*anna sat on the exam table, cursing herself. Her throbbing ankle was going to wreak all kinds of havoc on her work schedule. And dammit, why had Rhys been there when she'd face-planted? Now not only hadn't she proved that she was just as capable at extreme sports as he was, she'd utterly embarrassed herself, too.

"Hey, you," Rhys said as he strode back into the exam room holding two paper coffee cups from a local café. "Faith brought these for us. She took the time to head down to Roosters instead of grabbing the sludge from the cafeteria." He handed her one of the cups. "She had to get back to Keating Hollow to pick Zoey up from a friend's house. She said to call her later to let her know how you're doing and that she'd drop your car at your place and just walk home."

"Okay." Zoey was Faith's soon-to-be stepdaughter. Hunter must've been working. Hanna closed her eyes and leaned back on the table. A tech had already taken her in for an X-ray, and now they were just waiting for the results.

"How's it feel?" Rhys asked, sitting down next to her.

She shook her head. It hurt like hell, but dwelling on it only made it worse. Talking distracted her from the pain. "What were you doing at the drop zone?"

Rhys let out a sigh. "Just watching. I'd just got done with a sunrise hang gliding session and…" He shrugged. "I probably should've just gone home, but I wanted to make sure you landed safely."

Hanna turned and met his gaze. "I guess it's a good thing. Turns out I *do* need someone to babysit me."

He took her hand between both of his. "You definitely don't need a babysitter, love. But I am glad I was there. You can't drive no matter what the diagnosis." They both glanced at her right leg that was wrapped up in a bandage and an ice pack. "I'm sorry if I overstepped."

The truth was Hanna was pissed he'd followed them. It made her feel like he didn't trust her to take care of herself. On the other hand, she was so grateful he was there to take care of her. He always knew just what to do or say to comfort her. She just wished it wasn't necessary at all. "I'm glad you're here."

He rewarded her with a sweet smile and dipped his head to give her a soft kiss on the back of her hand. "Me, too, Han."

The door swung open, and the tall, redheaded doctor strolled in. She flashed Hanna a brilliant smile. "Good news, Ms. Pelsh. No break."

Hanna let out a sigh of relief. "That *is* good news."

"The bad news is it's a pretty intense sprain." She held up an X-ray to the light. "We'll send you home with an air cast. Stay off it until the swelling goes down and you can put your weight on it without much pain. The in-house healer has a salve for you that will do good things for the inflammation. Use that twice a day. Once the pain is manageable and you can move it, there are exercises for you to do to promote healing and range of motion. Any questions?"

"Yeah," Hanna said. "How am I supposed to work? I'm a baker."

The doctor gave her a sympathetic smile. "Sit on a stool with your foot up and direct someone else to do the manual labor."

Hanna pressed her palm to her forehead. "Oh, gods. My mom is going to *love* this."

"Is Mom a little overprotective?" the doctor asked.

"No." Hanna grimaced. "She's my business partner."

The doctor winced. "Need a note?"

That got a chuckle out of Hanna. "No, but thank you for the offer. We'll work it out. Maybe I can bribe my cousin to put in more hours."

"Do what you have to, Hanna. Just don't mess around with that foot. If you don't give it time to heal, you could do some permanent damage."

"I'll make sure she stays off it," Rhys said, squeezing her hand. "Even if I have to bake her cookies myself."

Hanna snorted. "Sure, Rhys. Like you have time to do my job, too."

He winked at her. "The pub isn't open at five in the morning, is it?"

"No but—"

"Friends, remember? It's what we do."

"This one's a keeper," the doctor said, grinning at Rhys. "Easy on the eyes, too." She made a note in her file while Hanna silently wished for the floor to open up and swallow her. When the doctor looked up, she said, "I'll have the nurse bring in the salve and some herbs for the pain and inflammation. Then you're free to go. Don't hesitate to come back in if you don't start to see some improvement within the next five or six days. Got it?"

"Got it." Hanna tried to wiggle her toes and winced. They

were swollen, and they looked and felt like overstuffed sausages.

The doctor walked out, leaving her and Rhys alone again.

She glanced at his handsome face and bit back a sigh.

"What?" he asked, raising one eyebrow. "Don't tell me you don't want my help. I'm good at taking direction."

She snorted. "No, you aren't. Didn't I tell you I needed some space?" The words were an accusation, but she smiled at him and added, "And yet, there you were, ready to rescue me when I made an ass of myself."

His lips twitched, and Hanna could tell he was trying to suppress a grin. "I was just surprised to see you getting on that bus. That will teach me not to tell you there's something you can't do."

"I guess so." She laughed. But then their eyes locked, and silence fell between them. Hanna suddenly found it difficult to breathe. Butterflies fluttered in her stomach while gooseflesh popped out on her arms the way it always did when sparks danced between them.

"Damn, Hanna," he said, his voice so rough she actually shivered. "Are you cold?"

She shook her head, her hand tightening on his.

He broke their eye contact and glanced down at their entwined fingers. When he met her gaze again, he said, "It looks like no matter what I do or say, we always end up right back here."

Hanna actually chuckled. "I hope you don't mean the hospital."

He glanced around the room and slowly shook his head. Then he leaned in and gently brushed his lips over hers.

Every thought fled Hanna's head. All she knew in that moment was Rhys—his slightly earthy scent, his soft lips, his rough hand caressing her cheek. *Mine*, she thought. This was what she wanted. What she'd always wanted. She lifted her free hand and pressed it against his muscular chest while he deepened the kiss. He tasted of coffee and a hint of maple syrup and love.

"Hanna," he whispered against her lips and pressed his forehead to hers. "What are we doing?"

"Kissing. I'm pretty sure you're familiar with the concept." She smiled and ran her tongue over his bottom lip.

He let out a small groan and claimed her again. The kiss was hot and needy, and if her ankle wasn't still throbbing, Hanna was sure she would've sat up and wrapped her legs around him.

But it was a good thing she didn't, otherwise when the door swung open a second later, they would've been in a compromising position.

"Hello, hello," the nurse said, smiling at them and holding a white paper bag. "How's it going, Hanna?"

"Um, okay," she said, brushing her fingertips over her lips.

"Looks like I might've interrupted a little something, huh? No matter. That's one way to get your mind off the pain." The nurse laughed to herself and handed the bag to Rhys. "There are instructions for physical therapy, a salve for the ankle, and herbs for the pain. Make sure you take the herbs two or three times a day as needed until the pain subsides."

"Okay," Hanna said, thankful her breathing was back under control. "Thanks."

She pulled the wheelchair around and looked at Rhys. "Can you help your girlfriend into the chair and meet me out in the lobby? I'm going to find some crutches."

Hanna half expected Rhys to correct her on the girlfriend assumption, but he just nodded. "Sure. No problem."

As the nurse left the room, Rhys looked at her. "Ready to go?"

"Yep. How should we do this?" She started to scoot to the end of the exam table, but Rhys just scooped her up as if she weighed nothing. "Whoa. Okay. I know you carried me to your Jeep, but I could've hopped on one foot to the chair."

"Nah. I've got you." He smiled down at her and positioned them so that all she had to do was put her good foot on the floor and then ease down into the chair. "See," he said, supporting her weight as she leaned back and sat down. "Perfect. I think we make a good team."

"I think you were doing all the work," Hanna said.

"You'll be there for me next time." He placed the bag in her lap and then wheeled her out of the room.

"You're right. I will." That warmth came rushing back and even though Hanna's ankle was still making her grit her teeth, she was having a hard time being upset about it.

Just as they were about to roll through the glass doors, Healer Snow walked in.

"Hanna!" the healer exclaimed. "What happened? Nothing serious I hope?"

Hanna winced. "The ground jumped up and bit me. Just a sprained ankle. I'll survive."

"I'm sorry to hear that." Snow nodded and eyed the bandage. "Did they give you the salve that helps it heal faster?"

"They sure did." Hanna held up the bag. "And some herbs."

"Perfect." The healer pursed her lips as if in thought. "Anything else?"

"No. Why?"

A smile broke out over her pretty face, reaching her wide dark eyes. "Good. If you were on anything else, it might be a conflict. But if you don't have to take anything else, we should be good."

"Good for what?" Rhys asked.

"Healer Snow is working on a cure for the autoimmune disease that Charlotte had," Hanna said, referring to the disease that took her sister. It was a relatively rare condition that only affected about one percent of witches, but there'd been a slight uptick in the past ten years. Healer Snow had recently made it her mission to try to find a cure. "Since I share her DNA and carry the same gene, my blood is a good candidate for the trials."

Snow glanced over at him and smiled. "Hey, Rhys. Good to see you. How are you feeling?"

"Fine." His tone was clipped and a little guarded. Then he turned to Hanna, his eyes darker than normal and his mouth tight. "What do you mean a carrier for the same gene?"

Healer Snow put a soft hand on his arm. "Maybe this isn't the right place to discuss this?"

"No, it's fine," Hanna said, frowning up at Rhys. "It just means the autoimmune disease is dormant. I don't have any of her symptoms and I'm completely fine, but some day that could change. I've been doing these trials for the last year. Can't hurt, right?"

"You have the same gene?" Rhys asked again as if he was having trouble understanding.

"Yeah," Hanna said. "That can't be a surprise. She was my sister."

"I... right," he said, straightening his shoulders. "Of course. I just never considered..." He shook his head. "Sorry. That just took me by surprise."

Hanna patted his hand. "It's okay, adventure boy. I'm fine. Perfectly healthy, other than the ankle, and that isn't life threatening."

Rhys held her gaze for a long moment, as if trying to make sure she was telling him the whole truth. Finally, he nodded. "Good."

Healer Snow was staring at him with her eyebrows pinched together. "Rhys? Can I talk to you for a moment?"

He stiffened, and Hanna fully expected him to question why she wanted to talk, but he just nodded and followed her over to a deserted corner. Healer Snow pressed a hand to his wrist and started to count to herself. Hanna had experienced the same routine every time she came in for a checkup or a trial. It was the healer's way of checking energy levels. The fact that she was checking Rhys made Hanna nervous. Why would she do that now? What was going on?

Hanna fretted as she watched them talk, and once they were done, Healer Snow pulled out her prescription pad, scribbled something, and handed it to Rhys. He started to make his way toward Hanna, but Snow put her hand on his arm and stopped him again.

Eventually Rhys nodded, shoved the prescription in his pocket, and then had the nerve to paste a fake smile on as he approached Hanna.

"What was that about?" she asked.

Rhys pushed her chair toward the door. "She thought my energy levels seemed low. I have a prescription for some herbs that are supposed to boost my immunity or something."

Hanna craned her neck to look at him. "Are you a patient of hers?"

He didn't answer as he rolled her outside.

"Rhys?"

He stopped at the passenger side of his Jeep and opened the door. When he turned to her, he said, "Healer Snow was my dad's doctor."

"Oh." All of Hanna's irritation and suspicion fled. She knew how close Rhys had been with his dad and just how devastated he'd been when his father had suddenly passed when Rhys was only fourteen years old. That experience was likely the reason that he'd been the only one who'd known what she needed after they lost Charlotte. "I'm sorry."

"There's nothing to be sorry about, Hanna," he said softly. "Now raise your arms so I can get you into this Jeep."

"I know." She lifted her arms in the air. "I just don't like seeing you sad."

He picked her up, cradling her against his chest. "I'm not sad, pretty girl. It's just been quite the morning. Ready to go home and get some lunch?"

She wrapped her arms around his neck and leaned in, giving him a kiss on his cheek. "Yes. And if I forgot to say so, thanks for being here for me. You've made it almost bearable."

"Anytime, Muffin. You know that." He gently set her in the Jeep and helped her prop her foot up. Then he buckled her in and took her home.

CHAPTER 9

    aith Townsend stared down at Hanna's ankle, her hands hovering just over the swollen flesh. They were at Faith's spa, and Hanna was there for a massage, but before they got started, she'd asked Faith if there was anything she could do to help her ankle heal faster. "Probably." Faith said. "But are you sure you want me to try this? I'm still not entirely sure what happened that day in the hospital with my dad. I just... I don't know, provided an outlet for his pain?"

A few months earlier, Faith's father had suffered a serious respiratory infection while recovering from chemotherapy and was in the hospital. Faith, as a water witch, didn't have the ability to craft herbs or potions the way her sister Abby did, but she was able to manipulate fluid, and whatever she'd done that day in her father's hospital room, everyone had sworn she'd helped to speed up his healing.

"Just try," Hanna said, trying not to beg. She was fed up with everyone babying her. "If I have to sit on the stool one more day and watch Candy use the wrong measuring cup for my scones, I'm going to scream."

"That bad, huh? What happened to Rhys?" Faith asked. "I thought you said he offered to help."

"He did. Actually, he came by on Monday, but I sent him away." When he'd dropped her off at home on Sunday afternoon, he'd been distant, like he was lost in his own thoughts. And instead of kissing her goodbye, he'd just squeezed her hand and said he'd see her in the morning. It had been a pretty major letdown after their make-out session in the exam room. She knew then he'd regretted his actions and didn't want a situation where he needed to let her down easy again. "Candy was there, and I told him he could go. He already has a job. He doesn't need to be doing mine."

Faith stared at her friend, looking exasperated. "Seriously?"

Hanna threw her hands up. "What do you want me to do, Faith? Let him hang out in my café and torture me with the 'friend' talk again?"

Faith pulled a stool over to the massage table and sat down next to Hanna. "Is that what he said? Even after the kiss on Sunday at the hospital?" After Hanna reluctantly cancelled her date with Chad, she'd called Faith Sunday night and filled her in on all the gory details.

"No, but that was coming. If it wasn't, he'd have called by now." Hanna laid back on the table, rested her arm over her eyes, and blinked back the tears that were threatening to fall. "I know he's attracted to me, but for some reason, he's dead set against dating me. I can't take it anymore, Faith. It's torture. So I sent him away."

"Oh, Hanna," Faith said. "I'm sorry, honey."

Hanna sucked in a stabilizing breath and sat up. "I know. I just have to let this go. It's not going to happen, and expecting it to is just killing me. So I've made a decision."

Faith raised her eyebrows. "Please tell me you're going to let Chad take you out on a real date."

Hanna gave her a tight smile. "No. We had a date for Sunday, but I canceled after I hurt my ankle. But now, I think it's just a bad idea to reschedule. I can't do that to him. He already knows Rhys and I have this weird thing. It's not fair to drag him into the middle of it."

"Oh." Faith slumped. "That's too bad. He's hot."

"You can say that again," Hanna said with a laugh. "I'm giving up Rhys. No more pining, no more letting him intrude on my thoughts. And I'm going to join one of those dating sites, see how it goes. Find a rebound guy or something."

Faith frowned at her. "How exactly is that different from dating Chad?"

Hanna shrugged. "Chad isn't a rebound guy. He's the type you take home to meet the parents. He's charming, talented, and really, really hot. Definitely not a rebound guy."

Chuckling, Faith nodded. "Yeah. I see your point." She stood and rubbed her hands together. "Okay, I'm going to see what I can do with this foot, and then after that you're going to let me help you with your online dating profile."

"Sure. Why not?"

"I'm going to step out while you get under the sheet," Faith said. "Just toss the robe over onto the chair."

"Please. You don't have to leave. How many times have you seen me change my clothes in my lifetime? Just stand here so I can use your shoulder for balance as I get under this sheet."

"So much for being professional," Faith said with a wink. "But the customer is always, right, I guess."

"Quoted for truth," Hanna said, grinning at her as she hauled herself up onto her good leg, and dropped the robe. A few moments later, she managed to squirm her way under the sheet, but ended up on her back instead of her stomach. "You'll need to work on the ankle first. If I turn over, I'm going to have to hang my foot off the table."

"I'm on it," Faith said. "Just relax."

"I'm trying to relax," Hanna said, slightly exasperated. "Why do you think I came here?"

They bantered back and forth for the next twenty minutes while Faith lightly trailed her fingers over Hanna's foot. Her touch was warm and slightly tingly. Hanna had been prepared for the treatment to hurt, but instead it actually felt good. Hanna could've laid there the rest of the afternoon, luxuriating in the experience.

"Can I try something?" Faith asked.

"Hmm? Sure," Hanna said.

"Don't you want to know what I'm going to do?"

"I trust you." Hanna was floating. Faith hadn't even started massaging yet, and already her tension was fading away. She felt Faith lift her foot and gently poke at the sore areas. Only they hurt less than they used to, and Hanna didn't even flinch.

"Good," Faith said. "How does this feel?" She gently rotated Hanna's ankle, testing the movement.

"Wow." Hanna sucked in a long breath. "It's stiff, but it doesn't hurt."

"Excellent!" Faith repeated the motion a few times and then tucked her foot back under the sheet. "Okay, now that we're done with that, I want to ask you a favor."

Hanna opened her eyes and peered at her friend. "You have me in a compromising position."

Faith gave her an evil grin. "I know. That's the beauty of it. If you were a paying customer…"

"What is it?" Hanna asked with a chuckle.

"Would you mind if I let a possible new hire massage you as part of her interview process?"

"She's here now?"

"Yep." Faith sat back down on the stool. "You remember the one who looked good on paper?"

Hanna nodded.

"Okay, so she came in today, and she's cool. About a year of experience, but I don't know. I just got a vibe that I can't put my finger on. I don't know what to make of it."

"A bad vibe? A creepy vibe?" Hanna asked.

"No. I don't..." She shook her head. "It's not necessarily bad, I just need a second opinion. If she has great hands and you think she's cool, then I think I'll hire her, but if not..."

"I get it. Sure. Send her in."

"You're the best." Faith leaned down and gave her a quick hug."

"I'm naked under here," Hanna said dryly.

"So what? You're the one who doesn't care if I see you naked." She smirked and bounced out.

Hanna lifted her foot and gently rotated it. There was no pain, not a lot of resistance either. "Whoa," she whispered. Talk about magical hands. She had no idea how Faith had done it, but her foot had gone from a swollen, achy mess to something that she might even be able to hobble around on.

There was a soft knock at the door. "Hanna?" a sweet voice called.

"Yep. I'm ready."

The door popped open and a honey-blond woman with a heart-shaped face strolled in. She looked to be in her early-twenties, slender, with big green eyes and a smile that lit up the room. "Good afternoon, Hanna. I'm Luna. Is there anything I need to know before we get started?"

Hanna told her to be careful of her ankle, but other than that, she was good to go.

"Do you mind if I touch the bruised areas? I just want to get a feel for how bad it is, see if there's anything I can do to help."

"I guess so. But be careful. I just don't want to injure it again," Hanna said.

"No, we definitely don't want that. I'll be gentle." The therapist gently pressed her hand to the ankle, and Hanna knew she was in good hands. The woman's touch produced the same warmth and tingles she'd experienced with Faith. Maybe, just maybe, by the end of the session her ankle would be as good as new.

~

"WELL?" Faith asked. "I'm dying to find out how it went."

Hanna was sitting out on the luxurious patio Hunter had built behind the spa, sipping a glass of wine. She'd somehow managed to get dressed after the massage, but going anywhere else was out of the question. Every muscle had turned to jelly in the best possible way. "It was glorious. If you don't hire her, I will."

Faith laughed. "What are you going to do with a massage therapist at the café?"

"Chair massages? I don't know. Something. Those hands are magic." Hanna lifted her foot and started to write the alphabet exactly as she'd been instructed by Healer Snow. "Look. My range of motion is incredible. I think it might be better than before I sprained it."

Faith rolled her eyes. "You know that was me, right?"

"And her," Hanna insisted. "She did something very similar. I swear, Faith, she finished what you started."

"Really? Now that's interesting." Faith peered at her friend. "What did you think of her vibe? Did you like her?"

"Are you kidding? I love her. She reminds me of a cross of you and Abby. Or at least the version of Abby since she married Clay. I swear, that woman has so much joy. It should be illegal to smile that much."

Faith was silent as she mulled that over. "Huh. I think

you're right. She has the drive to take chances—she's doing that by moving to Keating Hollow, but she has that angel face that everyone loves, too, just like Abby." She frowned and rubbed at her forehead. "I just don't understand why I'm hesitating."

"Because you're afraid the clients will like her better?" Hanna said with a tilted smile.

"No," Faith said far too quickly.

Hanna gave her a reassuring glance. "Of course not, babe. I was just teasing. Relax. She's great, and now this magical place can have not one, but two amazing therapists. Embrace it."

Faith chewed on her bottom lip. "You really think she's cool?"

"Yes," Hanna said. "Hire her or else I'm finding a new masseuse."

"All right, fine. I'll do it." Faith threw her hands up in mock defeat. "I guess if my best friend gives her two solid thumbs-up, then that's a sign."

Hanna balled her hands into fists and gave Faith a cheesy grin as she flipped her thumbs up, just to be a pain. "You won't regret it. And think of the long lunches you can take with Hunter while Zoey is at school."

Faith rolled her eyes, but Hanna didn't miss the secret smile tugging at her lips. But when she noticed Hanna staring at her, Faith cleared her throat. "So, about that dating profile…"

CHAPTER 10

*T*he predawn light filtered in through the café's front window while Hanna leaned on one of her crutches, waiting for the mixer to do its thing. She gazed at the lobby space and contemplated what sort of display she might put together to liven the place up. During special events, like Halloween, her mother and father worked together to spell the coat rack, making it act as a butler of sorts that entertained patrons with its antics.

But Hanna wanted something a little marketable. Something tourists could see from the cobblestone walkway, that would bring them in even if they weren't exactly in the market for pastries and coffee. She had a vision of dancing cookies and fancy latte art. She could handle manipulating the latte art, but she'd need her mother for the dancing cookies.

The bell chimed on the front door just as the timer went off for the fresh batch of scones she'd tucked in the oven as soon as she'd arrived.

"Be right there," she called over her shoulder as she hobbled into the back room. Her ankle had made a remarkable improvement, but it was still weak, and she had to build up strength before she could ditch the crutch. At least she was getting around now and didn't need Candy until later in the day.

"What's in the oven?" she heard Rhys ask from behind her. "It smells amazing."

Her heart did a little jig, and she smiled to herself as she turned around and said, "Cinnamon maple." She waved at the tray she'd just slid into the cooling rack. "Fresh from the oven. Want one?"

"Hell yes." He strode into the back like he owned the place, but instead of making a beeline for the scones, he stopped right in front of her and leaned down to place a soft kiss on her lips.

She was so shocked, she just stood there like an idiot, blinking up at him.

"Good morning, Hanna." His voice was gruff and his hand slightly calloused as he cupped her cheek. And not for the first time, she wondered what he did exactly that made his hands rough. He worked at a bar, not a construction site.

"Morning," she said, pressing her hand to his. "Rhys?"

"Yeah." His warm lips brushed over hers again, making her body tingle from head to toe.

"Where do your callouses come from?" She gently pulled his hand away from her face and ran a hand over the rough parts of his palm and fingertips.

He gave her a strange look as if he couldn't believe she was asking that question. "Where do you think they come from?"

"I honestly have no idea," she said, lifting his palm and placing a kiss right in the middle. "Pub work doesn't seem like it would be that hard on one's hands."

His eyes closed, and he let out a slow breath. "No. You're right, it doesn't. But chopping wood does."

An image flashed in her mind of him shirtless in just a pair of low-slung jeans while he wielded an ax, and she nearly groaned. Holy hell, the thought was almost enough to make her combust. "You chop wood?"

He let out a low chuckle. "Almost every morning. Where do you think your parents got that stash of split logs from last fall?"

"What?" She jerked back so that she could look up at him. "I knew you delivered it for them, but I didn't know you chopped it, too."

"How else do you think I keep in shape." He lifted one glorious arm and flexed for her, once again showing off that forearm.

"The gym?"

He laughed. "Sometimes. But I enjoy the solitude of chopping in my backyard."

She studied him for a moment. "When exactly did you start this chopping? You never did that before."

He shrugged one shoulder. "A little over a year ago."

So, he'd started that after they'd stopped dating. Interesting. "Well, Rhys, keep me in mind if you find yourself with more wood than you can handle."

A gleam lit his dark gaze, and he moved in, trapping her between his body and the counter. "Are you in the market for some wood, Hanna?"

Her gaze involuntarily dropped to below his waistline, and she felt her cheeks heat.

"Let me rephrase," he said, his voice gruff. "Are you in the market for *my* wood."

She was. Goddess above, she definitely was. But if she let herself go there, no doubt she'd get burned. This was a dangerous game he was playing, and if they ever actually got naked together, it would have to be for keeps. With him, there wasn't any halfway. She'd never survive it. "You're being vulgar, Rhys," she said softly even as she licked her lips.

"I'm not saying anything you aren't thinking, Han." He brushed one of her dark curls out of her eyes, and without another word, he pressed his lips to hers and kissed her with such fire, she felt every last one of her nerve endings come alive. And the wood in question pressed against her belly, his body straining for hers. She clung to him, meeting his earnest kiss with a passion of her own.

Mine, her mind said again, and she wrapped her arms around him, pulling him in closer.

Rhys let out a low groan and deepened the kiss, both of his rough hands gently cradling her cheeks.

She loved the feel of him, wanted to wrap herself around him and get lost for hours.

"Hello?" a voice called from the café. "Hanna, are you here?"

"Damn," Rhys muttered, backing off. He was breathing heavily, and his face was flushed with desire.

"Be out in a sec!" Hanna called, her voice higher than usual as she panicked slightly from the hot make-out session in the back room. What if Candy or her mother had walked in? They'd been fully clothed, sure, but there was no denying the way they'd been trying to fuse themselves together.

He let out a small chuckle and gently kissed her again. "Go. I need a minute to get control of myself." Both of them glanced down at the obvious bulge in his pants.

"Sorry?" Hanna said.

Rhys gave her a wry smile. "I'm not."

The door swung wide as Hanna hurried back into the front of the café as fast as her crutch would allow. A small line had formed, and she winced. Damn. She hated making her customers wait. But she sure hadn't hated the reason.

"Baking must be taking it out of you today," Barb Garber said, blinking at her. "You look a little warm."

Hanna cleared her throat. "The crutch and the ovens definitely keep me warm."

"You need help, dear," Barb added, her face scrunched up in concern. "You shouldn't be the only one here with that foot the way it is."

"Oh, I have help. He'll be out in a minute. We just had an oven situation to deal with. What can I get for you?"

She rattled off an order for a mocha and a latte and took her sweet time deciding on her pastries while Hanna expertly concocted the drinks. By the time she was pouring the milk into the cups, Rhys walked out of the back, looking as cool as could be. And then he jumped on the register, taking orders and pulling pastries as if he was a regular employee.

In no time, the line was gone and it was just them again.

"Here." Rhys pulled her stool over to the counter. "Take a seat. I'll restock."

"Rhys," she said, grabbing his arm to stop him. "I appreciate that you're here and all, but you shouldn't be doing this. Don't you have to be at the brewery in a few hours?"

"Yes, but by then Candy and your mom will be here. Don't worry. I like helping you."

Hanna frowned and glanced at the clock. "Candy was supposed to be here a half hour ago." She started to reach for her phone to call her cousin, but Rhys's words stopped her.

"I told her I'd cover her," he said. "She's sleeping off a long night of studying." The teenager had just started college that semester, and between helping out at the café and taking a full load, she was one busy girl.

Hanna paused. "Did she call you this morning?"

"Yep." He winked at her as he wiped down the counter. "I was more than happy to fill in. You know that."

She sighed. "I'm sorry. She shouldn't have done that."

"Hey." He walked over to her and wrapped his hands around hers. "Since when am I not allowed to help you out? You'd do it for me, right?"

"Yes, but—"

"No buts. I want to help. I wanted to help on Monday, and I would've been here Tuesday and Wednesday, too, if you would've let me." He ran a finger along her jawline. "And we both know you would've thrown me out with Candy here. I saw my chance, and I took it. I'd do it again in a heartbeat."

Hanna shook her head at him. "You're impossible, you know that?"

"How do you mean?" He stared down at her, his eyes searching hers.

"I never know what to expect. One minute we're friends. Then we're more. Then we're nothing. Next thing I know, we're kissing and then fighting, and…" She squeezed her eyes shut, praying she wouldn't cry. "And now you're acting like there's more between us, and I can't trust that. It always ends in heartbreak."

The door swung open, and Chad walked in.

Hanna sprang apart from Rhys and moved down the counter to the cash register, smiling brightly at the gorgeous man.

Chad's eyes lit up when he saw her. "Good morning, gorgeous."

Hanna heard Rhys let out a low grunt before his footsteps faded away as he disappeared into the back. He was either bailing after her outburst or putting another tray of scones in the oven. Hanna didn't know which and wasn't even sure she wanted to know. If he left after all of that, she'd have to hunt him down and kick him in the nuts.

"Morning," she said to Chad. "What can I get for you this morning?"

"Large black coffee, blueberry muffin, two chocolate chip cookies, and a date for Friday night."

Hanna's mouth dropped open in surprise. "A date?"

There was a loud crash from the back room that made Hanna jump, but she didn't move to find out what had happened.

"Yes. I need a date for a charity thing in Eureka, and I thought—"

"Sorry. Hanna already has plans for Friday," Rhys said, striding in from the back room, a tray of the cinnamon maple scones in his hands.

Hanna whipped around and gave him a questioning glance. "I do?"

"Yes. With me. It's what I was trying to tell you earlier, when we were in the back room." Those chiseled cheeks of his actually flushed as he said the words, and it made Hanna warm all over. She held one finger up to Chad. "Give me just a second?"

Chad was frowning in Rhys's direction, but he nodded. "Take all the time you need."

Hanna moved as fast as she could to Rhys's side and whispered, "What the hell are you talking about?"

He put the tray on the counter and leaned in. "Our date for Friday night. I already have it all set up, I just didn't get a chance to ask you yet. And no way am I letting that Ken Doll get you for the evening. I have plans. *We* have plans. That is if you don't hate me. I know I've been a..."

"A challenge?" Hanna finished for him with a soft smile.

"Yeah. A challenge." He gave her a sheepish grin. "I hope you won't hold it against me."

She rolled her eyes and then shook her head. But she said, "I probably will for at least a little while."

"You wouldn't be my girl if you didn't."

She had to hold back a sigh. He'd said *my girl* and meant it. Hanna wanted to throw herself in his arms and kiss him with everything she had, but Chad was still standing at the register, scowling at them. "All right. I need to go let him down easy now."

"You do that." But instead of letting her go, he grabbed her hand and pressed a soft kiss to her temple first.

"Rhys," she warned. "I'm working."

He chuckled. "So am I."

She rolled her eyes at him and then returned to the front counter where she began pouring Chad's coffees. "I'm sorry, Chad. I wish I could help you out, but it appears I do already have plans with Rhys over there."

Chad cast Rhys an irritated glance but then shrugged it off and said, "No problem. Except I'm not sure who else to ask. All of the Townsend sisters are spoken for, right?"

She laughed. "Yep. Let's see. You could try Shannon at the chocolate shop, Lena at the spa, or even the new girl that just started working there. Her name is Luna."

"Luna and Lena?" he asked, chuckling.

"They aren't connected in any way. Luna is a blonde like you, kinda on the tall side and with delicate features. Lena is a gorgeous, petite Latina woman. Just depends on your type."

"I see. Well, thanks for pointing me to the eligible females of the town. Do you recommend one over the other?" Chad asked, leaning on his elbow on the counter.

"It depends on if you like sweet, sassy, or sexy," Hanna said.

"Hmm, a combination sounds good," he said with a laugh.

Hanna threw her hands up. "I'm not navigating that one. Lena is sassy, Luna appears to be really sweet, though I just met her, and Shannon is a strong, sexy chocolatier. And that's all I've got for you."

Chad nodded. "Maybe I need to get some chocolate and then have a massage today."

"Probably not a bad plan." Hanna handed him his order, made change for his twenty, and said, "Sorry I couldn't make it. I usually enjoy benefits. Are you going to play the piano?"

He nodded. "Just a few songs."

"I'm sorry I'll miss that," Hanna said, meaning it. She liked Chad. If it weren't for Rhys and all their history, she could see starting up something with him. "Whoever you ask is a lucky girl."

"Thanks, Hanna. Have a good date."

She gave him a shy smile. "Thanks."

Chad left without looking back and as soon as the bell chimed indicating he was gone, Rhys was there again, slipping his arms around her from behind. "The date is going to be magical, love. Trust me."

She leaned back against his chest and sucked in a deep breath. If it was with Rhys, for her there was no question. As long as he didn't push her away, it *would* be magical. Any date with Rhys always made her tingle inside. "Does this mean I should delete my online dating profile?"

"You have a dating profile? Since when?" Rhys asked.

"Does it matter?"

"Not really." He walked over to the laptop on the counter. "Let's see it."

"What? No." She shook her head. "No way."

"Come on, Muffin. I want to see who's been hitting on my girl."

"Stop calling me Muffin."

"I will if you let me see that profile."

It might be worth it, she thought. Besides, she knew he wasn't going to let this go. With a shrug, she pulled up the website and tapped into her account.

"Whoa. Looks like I have some serious competition here. This guy is forty-eight, at least forty pounds overweight, and likes to spend his days antiquing. Right up your alley, no?"

Hanna swatted him. "You know I hate antiquing."

"That's your only objection? It says here he likes to hunt, too. Poor Bambi."

"Stop! Obviously he's not the one," she said.

"How about this one? He's twenty-two and looking for a poly relationship. Sounds crowded."

Hanna giggled. "Sharing is caring, right?"

He swept his gaze over her, his attention lingering on her lips. "I don't share."

"What are you going to do about it?" she challenged.

His lips twitched into a whisper of a smile as he clicked her user name and hit delete, erasing her account. "You won't be needing this anymore."

CHAPTER 11

*H*anna sat at the small table near the front window of her cream-colored cottage with the red shutters waiting for Rhys. Red, yellow, and violet flowers were blooming in her flower beds, and the small yard was perfectly manicured. It was everything she'd ever wanted for her home —classy, sweet, and full of beauty.

It was late in the afternoon when he hopped out of the driver's seat and trotted up to her red door. But before he could even knock, the door flew open and Hanna stood there wearing a romantic off-the-shoulder red blouse that showed off her bronze skin, dark blue jeans that she knew made his mouth water, and shimmering gold, strappy low heels. The heels that wouldn't kill her ankle and still made her feel sexy as hell.

"Good evening," she said with an almost shy smile as she scanned his choice for dinner-wear. Rhys had shown up in jeans and a black sweater that hugged his muscular frame. "Sweet holy pecs. Whoa," Hanna said, swallowing hard. "You look gorgeous."

"You don't look so bad yourself, beautiful." He swept his gaze down the length of her body and gave her a look that said it was all he could do to not walk her back into her house and carry her to her bedroom.

"Thanks." That look was almost enough for her to yank him inside, but she managed to keep her head as she grabbed a jacket off her coatrack and stepped all the way out onto the porch, closing the door behind her. "So. Where exactly are you taking me tonight, Mr. Silver?"

He opened the Jeep door for her and gave her a mysterious grin. "It's a surprise. I hope you aren't starving, because we have a stop to make first."

"I'm okay." She eyed him, as if trying to figure him out. "You're not taking me to one of those escape rooms, are you? Or maybe a murder mystery party?"

"Nope. I'm keeping you all to myself tonight." His voice was a little husky as he said the words.

Well, if that didn't just make her stomach flip with anticipation.

Rhys reached over and turned the stereo on. Lady Gaga and Bradley Cooper started singing their hit number "Shallow." The music washed over Hanna, giving her gooseflesh the way it always did when she heard it. Only now it was worse because she was enclosed in a vehicle with Rhys. Instead of reclaiming the wheel with his right hand, he slipped his fingers through hers and cradled her hand in his lap.

"Thanks for coming out with me, Hanna. I owe you a really good date," he said, his lips curving into a ghost of a smile.

"You're damned right you do." She squeezed his hand as she added, "I hope this lives up to the hype."

He chuckled. "I guess we'll find out soon enough."

Rhys steered the Jeep down the winding road that headed out toward the coast. As they rolled by the redwoods and hillsides, Hanna sat back in her seat and felt content for the first time in forever. She didn't let herself think about what would happen tomorrow, or when Rhys would change his mind, or what would happen if this didn't work out. They were together now, and all she wanted to do was enjoy it.

Once they got to Eureka, Rhys turned down highway 101, and before she knew it, he was making the turn that sent them out to the regional airport. Hanna turned to Rhys. "Is this a *Pretty Woman* moment? Should I have worn a ball gown for the opera in San Francisco or something?"

He snorted his amusement. "Do I look like an opera-type guy?"

"No," she admitted. "That seems more like Chad's thing."

He glanced over at her. "Do you wish you'd gone out with him instead?"

"Nope. Just trying to figure out what we're doing at the airport."

"You won't have to wait much longer, Miss Pelsh." He pulled the Jeep to a stop in the closest parking spot near an oversized hanger, and then jumped out to rush around and get her door for her.

"Thank you." She accepted his hand and felt like a princess as he helped her out of the vehicle. "You really know how to spoil a girl."

"You haven't seen anything yet, gorgeous." He slipped his arm around her, and together they walked slowly into the hanger.

"Hello, Mr. Silver," a man in a work shirt and jeans said. "The plane is just outside. A safety check has been done, and it's fueled up for your evening flight. You can take off as soon as you're ready."

"Thanks, John." Rhys glanced down at Hanna. "Come on. John is going to cart us out there." He tugged her over to a waiting golf cart, and the pair of them climbed into the back seat.

"This is unexpected," Hanna said with a nervous chuckle. She'd already figured out that Rhys was taking her on some sort of flight, but the plane they were headed for was really small. On the side it read *Skyhawk* and the tail had a Cessna logo. She didn't know much about planes, but she was pretty sure most of the people around the area used that type of plane when they were learning to fly.

"Are you nervous?" Rhys asked her.

"A little?" Saying she had butterflies would be putting it mildly. She felt more like crickets were jumping around in her stomach. She'd never been in a small personal aircraft before. "Is John our pilot?"

Rhys's grin widened. "Nope."

John stopped the golf cart next to the plane. "Enjoy your flight."

"Thanks. We will," Rhys said and helped Hanna onto her feet. He opened the door for her. "All aboard."

"You..." She stared at the front passenger seat of the small plane and swallowed hard. "You want me to sit there?"

"Yep."

"And you're the pilot?" Her voice cracked with nerves on the word pilot.

"You got it." He tucked her into the plane, closed the door, and ran around to the other side. Once he was in his seat, he strapped himself in and handed her a headset. "Buckle up and put this on."

Hanna sat there, frozen for a moment, trying to process this new information. "You learned to *fly*? When?"

"Over the last year. Don't worry. I have my pilot's license and have logged a lot of hours. You're in safe hands." He patted her knee. "But if you're too nervous we don't have to—"

"I'm good," Hanna blurted, excitement taking over. She was going up in a plane with Rhys. Talk about an adventure. Now that the shock had worn off, she was more than ready. "Let's go. Show me what you've got, Rhys. Impress me."

He grinned at her. "Well, we won't be doing any aerial tricks tonight, but I was hoping to let you catch the sunset over the Pacific. Will that do?"

"Absolutely. Let's do this." Hanna scanned the instruments in front of her on the dash. "But you don't need me to do anything, right? I mean, you've got this?"

"I've got this." He squeezed her knee lightly. "Just relax and enjoy the ride."

"Relax? Hell, I'm excited." Hanna leaned toward the window, peering out.

Rhys just laughed. "That's my girl."

Then he started the engine, and the propellers began to spin. Before she knew it, they were rolling down the runway and the plane took flight. Hanna felt her stomach drop with the sensation as they rose in the air. But she loved every bit of it. There was nothing better than the bird's-eye view of the northern California coast. There were mountains to the north and east of the them, the valley to the south, and the ocean to the west.

Rhys flew in a wide circle, making sure Hanna had a chance to take in everything she wanted to see, and then he turned the plane due west and headed toward the beach.

"It's just gorgeous, Rhys," Hanna said into the headset. "I don't think I can get enough of this."

"Want to head out over the ocean?" he asked.

Her answer was instantaneous. "Yes."

He chuckled again. "You got it."

The view was incredible, and Hanna couldn't resist pulling her phone out of her pocket to take a few pictures of the sun sinking into the Pacific. She felt free and alive and ridiculously happy that Rhys had known she'd love going up in the tiny plane. It really was the perfect date.

Hanna spent the rest of the flight glued to the window, taking pictures and marveling at the world below them. And then all too soon, he turned the plane around and started to head for the airport.

"Do we have to go back?" Hanna asked wistfully. "I love it up here."

"Sorry, love. We need to get back before we lose the light. I don't want to get caught up here in the dark."

"Okay. But I want to do this again... soon."

"You're on."

If Rhys hadn't indicated that he'd just recently gotten his pilot's license the year before, she'd have never guessed he hadn't had it for years. Everything about the flight was perfect —the take-off, the flying, and even the landing. And by the time they exited the plane, she decided she'd fallen just a little more in love with him. Not that she'd thought that was even possible, but her heart had swelled with love and admiration.

"You're incredible, you know that?" she said as he led her back to the Jeep.

"I was just thinking the same thing about you."

Hanna leaned against the Jeep and pulled him in close to her. "Rhys?"

"Yes?"

"This was wonderful. Thank you." Then she tilted her head and kissed him.

CHAPTER 12

*H*anna tasted of honey and fire and everything he'd ever wanted. The heady combination of feeling her lips against his and the adrenaline rush of the evening flight was enough to make him want to haul her off to the nearest hotel and show her just how much she meant to him. But even as he pressed his body to hers, he knew they had things to say first. After taking his time loving her with his lips, he pulled back.

"Ready for dinner?" he asked.

"I'm ready for something," she said breathlessly. "I'm just not sure it's food."

That amused him, and he smiled down at her as he brushed his fingers along her jawline. "Maybe not right here in the parking lot."

She glanced around as if just noticing where they were. "Right. Maybe we should get some food, since I'm clearly delirious with hunger."

"Is that the excuse you're going with?"

"It's as good as any," she said, her eyes twinkling with mischief.

"Can't argue with that." He opened her door and waited until she was safely in the passenger side.

Once he was in the Jeep and buckled up, he got them back on the road, headed toward her favorite sushi place in Eureka.

RHYS PULLED his Jeep into Hanna's driveway and killed the engine. Hanna had been full of commentary about the flight and her skydiving adventure all through dinner, but once they'd gotten back on the road, she quieted and appeared to be lost in thought. It was getting late, and he decided she'd just needed to wind down.

"Do you want to come in for coffee?" she asked.

Yes. He definitely wanted to follow her inside, but he was afraid that if he did, he wouldn't be leaving until the morning, and he really didn't want to mess this up. He'd spent years denying them both this relationship, and now that he'd decided to give it a try, he didn't want anything to ruin it. And that meant some honesty first. "How about we talk on that porch swing of yours?"

She raised one eyebrow, suspicion in her dark gaze. "You're not going to give me *the talk* again, are you?" There was fire in her eyes and a challenge in her voice that made Rhys itch to pull her into his arms. But then she drew in a breath and added, "Because if this date was always going to end with the same song, I don't need to hear it. I can just get out of this Jeep and we can go back to acting like we have over the last year, as if we don't know every little thing about each other and haven't been dancing around this thing between us for ten years."

Rhys zeroed in on 'know every little thing about each other.' He rolled the words over in his mind, knowing the statement wasn't true. They didn't know everything about each other. Not anymore anyway.

Hanna let out a heavy sigh and jerked the door open. "Thanks for the plane ride, Rhys." Her feet were on the ground and she was moving faster than she should considering her ankle was still a little weak, and Rhys knew he'd pissed her off. He hadn't been quick enough to reassure her he wasn't going to bail again.

He was out of the Jeep and by her side as she was trying and failing to shove her key in the lock. "Hey, Han. I'm not going anywhere. I promise."

She turned to him, her eyes full of fury. "I don't believe you."

Rhys took a step back, just as shocked as if she'd punched him.

They stared at each other for a couple of beats, neither of them blinking. Rhys needed her to see that he was there, that he wasn't running this time. He knew she didn't trust him. Not yet. But she would.

"Damn," Hanna said, breaking away first. She hung her head and whispered, "What do you want from me, Rhys? I don't understand."

He took her hand in his and gently tugged her over to the porch swing. Once he sat down, he pulled her into his lap, cradling her against his chest. "I want you, love. I always have. But there's a reason why I've been pushing you away. I think it's time you heard it."

She tilted her head just enough so that she could look into his eyes. But she didn't say anything; she just waited.

Damn, he thought. It was going to be a hell of a lot harder to tell her his truth while staring her in the eye, but he knew she deserved it. And she deserved to know it all. "Remember that day we were at the hospital and we ran into Healer Snow?"

"Sure."

"And you said something that I didn't know, something that made me question all of my assumptions about what I deserved in this life."

Her expression turned confused. "What didn't you know?"

He lifted his palm and cupped her cheek. "You told me you carry the same autoimmune gene that your sister had that caused her illness. I never knew that."

"You didn't?" She seemed shocked. "It wasn't a secret."

"When did you find out?" he asked her.

"I dunno. When I was in college I guess?" Her eyes widened, and she let out a low snicker. "I think it was when you were dating that annoying girl from Arcata. You know, the one who spoke with the fake British accent and acted like royalty?"

"She did live in the U.K. for four years. And she was distantly related to the queen if I recall," Rhys said, not sure why he was defending the chick who'd cheated on him with her brother's best friend.

"Please. She was no more related to the queen than I am," Hanna said with a snort. "In fact, her last name, the one she claimed tied her to the royal family, was from a stepfather."

Rhys laughed. "Yeah, okay. She was annoying. I'll give you that."

"Right. It also meant we weren't exactly spending a lot of time together. Morgan and I couldn't have been more different." She shook her head. "What *were* you thinking?"

Rhys let his fingers slide down her neck, and he kissed her softly on the lips before pulling back and smiling at her. "I was thinking temporary."

She blinked at him. "Temporary? That's not very kind."

"I never promised her anything, Hanna. I never promised

any of them anything. And when they started to want more than casual dating, I ended it. I had to."

"Why?" She tilted her head and looked at him so intently he was certain she was looking right into his soul.

"Because, love. I have the same gene that my dad and my grandfather had."

The words hung in the air between them while he let her absorb what he'd just said. They both knew that meant that he was a walking time bomb. The gene that ran in his family most often presented as a sudden heart attack. Usually a massive one that left little room for recovery.

Her expression went from total surprise, to shock, and then anger. "Dammit!" She jumped up off his lap and started to pace the porch. "All of this time, you knew, and you didn't tell me?"

Rhys draped his arm over the back of the swing and said, "I didn't know for sure, but I suspected. I found out for sure right before Christmas about fifteen months ago."

"Right before you told me we were better as friends." Her words weren't a question.

He answered anyway. "That's right. I couldn't risk it. In my mind, I was certain I only had a few years left on this earth. How could I in good conscience stay with you, knowing that I'd leave you, knowing I'd cause that bone-deep pain that never goes away? I watched my mom suffer. I didn't want to do that to you or any children we were blessed to have."

"Children?" she said with a small squeak.

He grinned at her. "Yeah, children."

"Whoa." She walked back over to the swing and sat down, but she didn't reach for him.

Rhys cursed himself. He'd said too much, too soon.

"I just need to know, Rhys," she said, turning to him. "Why the change of mind? Why now?"

He couldn't stand it. He needed to be touching her. As a

cool evening breeze picked up, he scooted closer and wrapped an arm around her, pulling her to his body. After giving her a soft kiss on the temple he said, "Because I learned that despite your genetic history, you're fearless. You've never let it stop you from doing anything, while I've been living only half a life. I figured if you could be brave, so could I. I'm done fighting it, Hanna. I want you and I love you. Always have. If you're still willing to give me a chance, I'm here, ready to see this through no matter what happens."

Tears filled her eyes, making them shiny as she tried to blink them back.

"Oh, Hanna." He pulled her into a hug, holding her tightly as he caressed her back. "It's all right. I'm sorry, honey. I should've told you sooner. I just didn't want to worry you."

She buried her face into his neck and made a muffled sound as she tried to talk.

"What's that?" he asked gently.

"You're a giant jerk," she said on a sob, but she still clung to him.

"I know."

"And I hate you," she added.

"I'm not surprised."

A chuckle reverberated through her chest, and she finally pulled back to look him in the eye again. Her eyes were sparkling with those unshed tears when she said, "You're an idiot."

"Why?" he asked curiously. "Because I wanted to protect you?"

"No. Because you failed to realize that I've been waiting for you this entire time and that as long as you were single, I was still going to wait. Isn't that pathetic?"

He shook his head, feeling that warmth in his chest again. "I think it's pretty romantic, actually."

"Romantic?" she scoffed. "More like insane. You should've wanted me to be happy, not a hot mess."

"I've always wanted you to be happy, Hanna. And if that meant someone else, I would've learned to live with it."

"Unless it was Chad. Then you probably would've kicked his ass."

That made him laugh. "Maybe. Chad just... he's too pretty and not nearly daring enough for you."

"You got that right, Mr. Silver." She slid off his lap and tugged him up to his feet. She wrapped her arms around his neck and said, "It's no secret that you're the one who holds my heart."

"That's good. Because if it was a secret, I'd probably be too dense to figure it out." He tugged her even closer until their bodies were melded together.

She nodded, making her gorgeous dark curls bounce. "I believe every word of that. Fortunately, I'm not that good of an actress."

"Hanna?"

"Yes, Rhys?"

"Tell me you forgive me."

"There's nothing to forgive. Not really. I understand." She tightened her hold on him. That old familiar pain was back in her eyes, reminding him of why he'd been so cautious in the first place. "But if you keep something like that from me again, we're going to throw down. Got it?"

"Got it." He dipped his head and kissed her. His heart ached with so much emotion he had to fight back tears. "I love you, Han."

"I love you, too." Her eyes were watery as she said the words and started to tug him toward the front door. "Come on. Let's go inside."

Rhys planted his feet and shook his head, ignoring his very

loud libido that was screaming for him to follow his woman into her pretty little cottage. "I can't, Hanna. Not tonight."

"Why?" She tilted her head to the side and studied him like he had three heads.

He nearly laughed at the thought. Instead, he cleared his throat and said, "I laid a lot on you tonight. I want you to have a chance to process it all before we take this to the next level."

"Are you seriously turning down sex so *I* can think?" Hanna asked incredulously. She was so cute with her outrage that he nearly picked her up and carried her into the house, damn the consequences.

"No, I'm pretty sure I have plenty of thinking to do, too," he said gently. "I just don't want to get in too deep until you have thought all this through. I don't want to risk what we have because we're too impatient."

"Rhys, dammit," Hanna said, wiping the single tear from her cheek. "Fine. No sleepovers yet. But be forewarned... they will be expected as this relationship moves forward."

"And thank the gods for that," Rhys said, moving in to kiss her goodnight one last time before he headed back to his cold and lonely bed.

CHAPTER 13

*H*anna hummed to herself as she decorated a batch of sugar cookies with the words, *Come on in. The coffee's more than fine.* She was careful to use the same script as the Incantation Café sign out front. After weeks of mulling over the idea to do a window display, Hanna was finally ready to get something going.

"What's got you in such a good mood today?" her mother asked from the doorway that led to the back room.

"I had a good date last night," Hanna said, adding a few fancy swirls to one of the cookies.

"You did? With who?" her mother asked. "Was it—"

"Hanna?" a voice called from the café.

"Hold on, Mom." Hanna brushed past her mother and spotted Noel Townsend standing in the lobby. Her face was glowing as if she'd just come from a facial, but Hanna knew Noel's newfound radiance had nothing to do with the spa and everything to do with the baby on board. "Look at you," Hanna said, rushing around the counter. "Look at that baby bump. I swear you weren't showing last week when you were in here. How many months is it now?"

"Just about four and a half months," Noel said with a grin. "And I was showing, but I was doing a fairly decent job of hiding it. Now, there's no disguising this girl." Noel pressed a hand to her abdomen. "She's letting everyone know she's coming."

"A girl?" Hanna said with a sigh. "Oh my gosh. Is your family allergic to the Y chromosome?"

Noel laughed. "It sure looks that way, doesn't it?"

"I'm so happy for you." Hanna gave her friend a big hug and felt the sting of happy tears burn her eyes. "Drew must be over the moon."

Noel squeezed Hanna's hands. "He is."

"He's always wanted kids, you know." Hanna bit her lower lip and tried not to think about what might have been. Drew and Charlotte had been high school sweethearts, and Drew had spent a lot of time at the Pelsh residence back in high school.

"I do," Noel said softly, holding Hanna's gaze. "She's still with him, you know."

Hanna's throat tightened, and dammit, one tear rolled down her face. "I'm sorry, Noel. This isn't fair to you. You and Drew, you're perfect together. You know I love and support you both, it's just that sometimes the past sneaks up on me and bites me in the ass, and I start thinking about what might have been had she lived."

"I know, sweetie. Trust me. I know. You think I don't sometimes wonder what might have been if Xavier hadn't disappeared? What my life and Daisy's life might have been like?" Noel was referring to her first husband and the fact that he'd disappeared one day, leaving her alone with her small child. He'd resurfaced recently, but by then it was too late for them. Too much had happened, and Noel was already in love with Drew. She gave Hanna a watery smile, her eyes tearing now, too. "We all loved Charlotte. She would've wanted us to go forward and be happy."

"You're right." Hanna pulled her into another hug. "I love you, and I can't wait to meet your new little one. Mixing your genes with Drew's means she's going to be the cutest thing that ever graced Keating Hollow."

"Until you and Rhys decide it's time to procreate," she said with a huge grin.

Hanna's face felt hot as she let out a nervous laugh. "Well, there's no chance of that yet. We haven't even um... you know."

"You will," Noel said with a wink. "You two have been dancing around this for years."

"I suppose." Hanna eyed her. "I guess this means Faith told you about our date."

She nodded. "First thing this morning while I was in for a foot massage. Have you met the new girl? Luna? Her hands are magic."

"Literally," Hanna said, rotating her ankle. "Between her and Faith, they should add healing services to the menu."

"I heard about that," Noel said with a nod and started to move toward the register where Candy was standing. The young girl was staring out the window, her eyes unfocused and a small dopey smile on her face.

Hanna waved a hand in front of her. "Hey, earth to Candy. You in there?"

Candy jerked and turned her attention to Noel. "Oh, oops. Sorry. I was thinking about a school project."

Noel raised one perfectly groomed eyebrow. "Must be some project. You looked more like you were reliving a hot one-night stand or something."

"Noel!" Candy cried and glanced around, no doubt looking

for her aunt. "Don't say things like that with Aunty Mary around. She talks too much."

Noel chuckled. "Sounds like I hit a nerve."

Candy scowled at her, and Hanna chuckled. Candy turned her fiery glare on her cousin. "Don't you start, too. I'm just trying to get through this day so I can—"

"Meet him at his dorm room?" Noel teased.

"Oh, stop. What do you want?" Candy demanded.

"Hot chocolate, extra whip." Noel put a five on the counter. "Keep the change for your condom budget."

Candy's mouth dropped open in a surprised "O." Then she rolled her eyes at Noel. "You people need better entertainment."

They both laughed. After Noel had her hot chocolate in hand, Hanna said, "Hey, can I borrow you for a minute?"

"Sure. I've got time before I need to pick up Daisy."

"Excellent. I'm working on a window display. I want to spruce it up like Hollow Books and A Spoon Full of Magic do with their front windows, but I need an air witch to help me out. Mom could do it, but she's been busy doing accounting stuff all week."

"Sure. What do you need?"

Hanna waved her over to the window all the way to the left that was behind the coffee condiment bar. "I want to create a floating display that highlights how to pour coffee art while cookies rise in the air around it. They have a welcoming message on them. I can handle spelling the liquid to do what it needs to do, but I need an air witch to spell the coffee cups and pitcher as well as the cookies to keep the display going. Do you think you can do that?"

"Sure." She furrowed her brow. "I think I'll need you to demonstrate the coffee art though, so I can spell the dishes to mimic your movements."

"Okay." Hanna moved the condiment bar out of the way and called over her shoulder, "Candy? Can you bring me a shot of espresso, a pitcher of steamed milk, and a mug?"

"Yep."

Hanna took a moment to clean up the window, and by the time she was done, Candy had her supplies ready. "Thanks."

With Noel standing next to her, Hanna used her considerable barista skills to demonstrate the latte art heart. She first poured the espresso into the cup and then lifted the pitcher up and down, slow, and fast, until the espresso helped form a heart in the latte's foam top. The whole time she demonstrated, she felt the faint tingle of Noel's magic wrapping around her.

"Isn't that lovely," Noel said.

Hanna had let go of the espresso shot glass and pitcher, but due to Noel's magic, they kept repeating her movements on a thirty second interval. All Hanna had to do was spell the liquid to return to the shot glass and pitcher each time so that the scene would replay over and over.

"This is going to be perfect," Hanna said, clasping her hands together. All she had to do was think about the espresso and the milk separating back into the pitcher and shot glass and suddenly the window she'd envisioned had come alive. Now all she needed were the cookies. "I'll be right back."

Five minutes later, Hanna and Noel were outside, observing the café wares perform the coffee art and watching the cookies rise in the air to welcome patrons into the store. Noel had her hot chocolate while Hanna sipped on a chai latte.

"That's cool," a familiar male voice said from right behind Hanna.

She turned and grinned at Rhys. "Noel helped me."

"It's very well done." He nodded at Noel. "Maybe the brew pub needs something like that."

"Maybe. Talk to Clay." Hanna wrapped her arms around him just because she could and gave him a sweet kiss on the lips. "I was hoping I'd see you today."

"Oh, you'll be seeing me every day from now on, gorgeous," he said and tucked her against his chest, running a hand down her back.

Noel let out a contented sigh. "You two are just so perfect. I can't believe it took you this long to get it together."

Rhys glanced over at her and smiled. "You know what, Noel? Me neither. But now that I've overcome my severe case of dumbassery, I'm hoping Hanna won't hold it against me."

"Don't worry," Hanna said. "I think we're past that now. Just don't eff up again."

"Yes, love," he said softly, and this time when he kissed her there was nothing sweet about it.

When he finally pulled back, Noel fanned herself. "Holy hotness, batman. Did someone just turn the heat up or what? I think I need a cold shower." Then she winked at them. "Congrats, you two. See you later."

They waved as she walked off, her hot chocolate still in her hand.

"Need a coffee?" Hanna asked him.

"I need more of you, but since it appears half the town is staring at us, maybe we'll save that for later."

Hanna peered past him and noted that Shannon and Miss Maple were standing outside of A Spoonful of Magic watching them while Clarissa was pushing a gawking Pauly Putzner back into the sheriff's office. And then there was Ms. Betty. She was shuffling her way down the street, her eyes bugging out, and she was making a beeline straight for them.

"Uh-oh. If Ms. Betty gets her hands on your backside, you won't be able to sit for a week," she said, laughing. "Remember what she did to Jacob?"

Rhys groaned. Ms. Betty had gotten a little handsy with Yvette's significant other right after he'd moved to town and was known for making a multitude of inappropriate comments. "Let's get inside. Maybe she'll forget where she was headed."

Hanna laughed. "I'll save you if she doesn't."

They scurried inside, and Hanna got busy making him the decaf mocha he'd asked for.

"Decaf?" Mary Pelsh said with a tinge of judgment in her tone. "Since when have you started laying off the caffeine?" she asked Rhys.

"Healer's orders," he said with a smile. "How are you doing, Mrs. Pelsh?"

"Well, since you asked, Rhys," she said, sounding combative. "I've been better to tell you the truth."

"I'm sorry to hear that," Rhys said as Hanna hurried over.

"Mom?" Hanna asked, concerned. It was rare for her mother to be short with people. Graciousness was her thing and snapping at people was unheard of. "What's going on? You sound upset."

"I *am* upset." She scowled at both of them. "What do you think you're doing?"

Hanna and Rhys glanced at each other, both confused.

"I'm sorry, Mrs. Pelsh," Rhys started. "What do you mean? We were just outside talking to Noel—"

"I mean this." She waved a hand between the two of them. "So, what? You're a couple again?" She glared at Rhys then turned her attention to Hanna. "I can't believe you're letting him back into your life like this. He's only going to hurt you."

"Mom!" Hanna gasped, horrified her mother had called her out like that right in front of Rhys and the few customers they had in the café. "You don't know what you're talking about."

"Don't I?" She whipped back to Rhys. "Did you or did you

not dump my daughter and then proceed to ignore her for over a year until you decided you'd made a mistake?"

"I…" Rhys glanced at Hanna and grimaced.

"Well?" Mary demanded.

"Rhys, you don't owe her any explanations," Hanna said softly. What was wrong with her mother? Hadn't she been thrilled when they went out to dinner just before she sprained her ankle? Hanna had no idea why her mother had done a one-eighty. She raised her voice and added, "Mother, we'll talk about this at home. In *private.*"

But Rhys and her mother were still staring at each other, Mary with her arms crossed over her chest and Rhys standing straight with his head high. His expression turned determined as he said, "I love your daughter, Mrs. Pelsh. I know I've made mistakes, and I've apologized to her. I can see now that I should have apologized to you as well. It was never my intention to hurt her. In fact, I was trying to protect her. Maybe—"

"I've heard enough," Mary said, her tone final. "Just know that I don't approve." She turned on her heel and stormed back into her office, slamming the door behind her.

Hanna jumped as the door rattled against the frame, and then she looked at Rhys helplessly. "I'm so sorry about that. I had no idea she'd behave that way. Hell, I had no idea she felt that way."

Rhys stared at the closed door and frowned. "I guess I need to just give her time."

Hanna slipped her arm through his and guided him to the counter where Candy had left his decaf mocha. Once he had it in hand, she led him outside. "You know my mom loves you, right?"

He let out a small snort. "Sure. It just pours off her."

Hanna chuckled softly. "Mary Pelsh never gets worked up about anything except the people she loves."

"She loves you, Han," he said, tugging her away from the front windows of the café. When they were out of sight, he dipped his head and gave her a light kiss. "You're the common denominator here."

"Maybe, but you've been in my life since I was a teenager. She did love you and I know she does now. She's just mad. Let me talk to her. I'm sure this will blow over."

He sighed and pulled her in, resting his chin on her shoulder. "I sure hope so, love. Because the last thing I want to do is come between you and your mother."

Hanna hugged him, loving him even more for caring so much about her family. "You won't," she promised. "We just need to let her get used to us. When she sees you aren't going anywhere, she'll come around."

"All right." He pulled back and smiled down at her. "In the meantime, will you come by the pub for my dinner break tonight? I'd take you out, but I have to close."

Hanna had wondered how their schedules were going to work. She normally opened the café, and he spent three or four days a week closing the brew pub. A slow smile claimed her lips. "I'd love to."

CHAPTER 14

"Mom!" Hanna tore through her parent's living room, livid at her mother. The way she'd treated Rhys was just downright rude and unacceptable.

"In here, Hanna," her mother called from the kitchen in the back of the house.

Hanna stormed in and stopped dead in her tracks when she spotted her mother with her head down on the table, a used tissue clutched in her hand. "Mom?" she said more gently as she sat next to her. "What's wrong?"

"Everything." Mary's head popped up and she looked at her daughter with red-rimmed eyes. "I was horrible today. I'm sorry."

"Oh, Mom." Hanna reached out and placed her hand over her mother's wrist. "It's all right. No permanent damage was done. I'm sure Rhys—"

Mary waved a hand. "I don't care what Rhys thinks, honey. I only care about upsetting you. I shouldn't have gone off like that in the store today. It was unprofessional. That's not what our customers have come to expect from us."

Hanna pulled her hand back and straightened, anger simmering in her gut again. "So, you're upset about the way our fight looked to customers?"

"Mostly I'm upset that I upset you," she said.

Hanna pushed her chair back and moved to the counter, where she started making a fresh pot of coffee just to keep her hands busy. After she flipped the switch on, she turned and stared at her mother. "What is your problem with Rhys?"

"He's not the right man for you." Her mother's tears were gone, and her expression was hard as steel.

"You don't get to make that decision, Mother," Hanna said, not backing down for a second. "Are you saying that your relationship with Daddy has always been sunshine and roses? That you've never had any ups and downs or doubts about whether you should be together? Rhys's only crime was trying to protect me."

Mary's eyes narrowed. "Protect you from what, exactly?"

"Getting hurt." Hanna threw her hands up in the air. "From falling in love with him, marrying him, and maybe even having his children and then losing him to the same heart condition that took his dad and his grandfather."

"Well, at least he got that part right." Mary stood up. "It's too bad he's not strong enough to stick with that position."

Hanna felt as if cold water had been dumped down her back. Did her mother really think Rhys should stay away from her because of what *might* happen in the future? "Is that what this is all about?" Hanna's voice was a little shaky as she added, "Are you saying Rhys doesn't deserve to be loved because of a condition he has no control over?"

Mary closed her eyes and sighed. "Hanna... Oh, honey. It sounds so awful when you say it like that. Of course, I don't think he doesn't deserve to be loved." She sat back down and patted the table with her palm. "Please, come sit with me and let me get this out. Then I swear, whatever you decide, I won't say another word."

Right, Hanna thought. But if she didn't sit and let her mother talk they were never going to be able to move past her mother's concerns. So Hanna took a deep breath, grabbed her coffee and sat next to her mother. "Okay. I'm listening."

"Rhys is one of the few people in this world who knows what it was like for you when we lost Charlotte," her mother started.

"Yeah? So? That's also because he was my one friend that was here for me when I really needed someone. He held me up, making sure I made it through the other side of my grief."

"I know." Mary's tone was milder now. "And I'm grateful to him for that."

"All right. So what's the problem? The real problem? Because I know it's not just because we broke up last year and had trouble keeping our friendship intact."

"It's selfish for him to want this with you, Hanna," her mother said. "His family history…" She shook her head. "Are you really telling me neither of you are concerned that you'll be moving ahead in your lives together and then one day he's just gone?"

"That could happen with anyone. It could happen to me. What if I develop Charlotte's autoimmune disease? Did you think of that? He could be the one stuck with a ticking time bomb." Hanna spoke stiffly, hating that her mother was reducing him to the gene he carried.

"That's not going to happen," she said, as if it was a ridiculous statement. "You've made it almost to your thirties without any indication of that illness. Healer Snow says it's very unlikely."

"Yeah. I know what Snow said. I also know that nothing is certain. She's never said I won't succumb to the disease. In fact, she's been careful to suggest that I need to keep my checkups current, because they never know when things might change."

Mary pressed a hand to her forehead. "Hanna, be serious. No one thinks you're going to end up with the disease. It's why you're a great control for Snow's tests."

"Fine. Whatever. I'm just saying that any of us could die at any moment. What if I get hit by a car or choke on a cashew? Does that make it unreasonable to fall in love, get married, have a kid or two?"

"No." Mary stood up and slammed her hand on the table. "But it is unreasonable for a man to take a wife knowing his heart is on borrowed time. I'm angry at him because this is going to hurt so much worse, Hanna. I just want to spare you that pain."

Hanna stared at her mother for a long time. Finally, she dropped her gaze to her folded hands resting on the table. "I heard you, Mom. What you haven't heard, or maybe just refuse to see, is that I already love him that much. It will hurt no matter what our relationship status is, so I'm choosing him no matter the outcome. I'd rather be by his side for as long as I'm allowed, even if it's just a few short years. That's my choice. And I've already made it."

"Fine." Mary's voice turned softer as she added, "But remember this conversation when this relationship moves forward and what it would mean for you and any children you have. What will your life look like if you lose him?"

Hanna's head snapped up, and she glared at her mother, hurt beyond words. "That was a terrible thing to say to me."

Tears sprang to Mary Pelsh's eyes as she said, "I know, honey. But it's a reality you have to face." Then she hurried into the hall, and Hanna was certain she heard her sob as her mother ran up the stairs.

~

"THANK YOU FOR COMING IN, HANNA," Healer Snow said as Hanna strolled into Snow's office. The woman had her dark hair pulled up in a smart twist, and she was wearing a bright pink silk blouse that said 'high-powered business woman' rather than 'earth-witch healer.' "Take a seat, please."

Hanna sat in an old gray office chair and rolled closer to the healer's desk. The space was small and a little stark with its white walls and metal desk. But Healer Snow had optimistic energy that lit up most rooms. She was the type who was certain that if she just kept peeking under the furniture and around corners that eventually they'd find effective treatments or cures for even the most misunderstood diseases. "So, is there a new trial you need me to participate in?"

Healer Snow had been working on the autoimmune disease that had taken Charlotte for over fifteen years. When Hanna found out they needed blood donors from people who carried the gene that was largely responsible for the disease, she'd signed up immediately. If there was anything she could do to save someone else from Charlotte's fate, she'd do it. Watching her sister live in pain and pretend to be perfectly fine so that she could enjoy the last days of her life had been torture.

Hanna had known just how sick Charlotte had been. She'd been there when Charlotte collapsed at night after she overdid it during the day just being a normal teenager. She'd witnessed the days when Charlotte couldn't get out of bed and the days when she forced herself to even when the bags under her eyes were so bad it looked like someone had beaten her.

But Charlotte hadn't let the illness hold her back. She'd lived and loved enough for an entire lifetime before she even graduated high school. And Hanna had been trying to emulate her ever since. Not that she'd had even a fraction of the challenges that Charlotte had. She just tried to remember that life was a gift and that to waste any of it on "what if" was an insult to Charlotte's memory.

"Yes," Snow said, nodding. "It's not just to take blood, though. This one is a human trial to see if a drug can change the markers of the underlying causes of the autoimmune disease."

Hanna frowned. "But I don't have the disease."

"That's correct. But as we discussed before, you do have the markers for it, meaning that if the production of the autoantibodies in your blood stream rises, you're at high risk for developing the disease. We want to use you as a control. See if your markers go down at all."

Most of this was over Hanna's head, but she trusted Healer Snow. "Would the drug make them go up?"

"Very unlikely. If it doesn't work the way we think it will, likely the medication will just flush out of your body."

Hanna shrugged. "Okay. Then sure. What do I need to do?"

"We'll need a full blood workup to make sure nothing's changed since your last checkup and then if all looks good, we'll start you on a low dose of the drug next week."

"Sounds good." Hanna stood and put her hand out to Snow. "Thank you for always pushing to learn more. My sister,"—her voice caught on the word *sister*— "she deserved more people like you in this world."

"And no doubt more people like you, Hanna. Thank you for always doing what you can for this research." Snow shook Hanna's hand with both of hers. "You're one of the angels around here."

Those tears stung Hanna's eyes again, but she blinked them back. "We all just do what we can."

"I suppose that's true." Healer Snow smiled at her. "Okay, have a good week. I'll see you at the next appointment."

"You, too." Hanna let herself out of Snow's office and headed to the lab.

CHAPTER 15

*R*hys sat on the plastic chair in the exam room waiting for Healer Snow as he stared at the exam table. He knew she'd ask him to sit on the end of it when she was ready to check his heart, but he wasn't going to speed up the process. Every time he heard the crinkle of the paper when he took his spot on the vinyl table, he pictured his father lying unconscious on the floor.

He supposed if he told Snow about that particular reaction, she'd recommend a head doctor. But he knew all he needed was a good hike, or swim, or a ride in that Skyhawk. Anything to clear his mind. Or maybe he just needed a date with Hanna. It'd been four days since her mother had blown up on her and since then, he'd only had dinner with her once. But that was about to change. He had the night off, and six o'clock couldn't come soon enough. He was itching to put his arms around her.

The door popped open, and Healer Snow walked in. She was wearing a bright pink filmy top and white pants, and he wondered how she managed to not get dirty within five minutes of getting dressed.

"Good morning," she said, pulling up a black rolling chair and taking a seat a few feet in front of him. "I hope I didn't keep you waiting too long."

"Morning." He gave her a reassuring smile. "I just got here a few minutes ago."

"That's very good, then. I love it when the day starts out on the right foot." She flipped open the folder she'd been carrying. "So, how have you been feeling since your last visit? Anything different? How's your energy level?"

"I've been feeling fine," he said. "I did have a former healer touch me and say my levels were below normal. I haven't noticed anything different, but I did pick up an energy potion at the local herb shop just in case."

She nodded. "Are you still running?"

"Yep."

"Hang gliding?"

"Sure. I just went last week."

"Surfing?"

He laughed. "Not in a few weeks."

"How about swimming? Last time we talked you were hitting the laps four times a week."

"Not as much swimming lately. But I have been hiking some in the redwoods."

"How many miles do you hike?" she asked, her pen already scrolling across the page.

"Depends on how much time I have, but usually five to ten miles roundtrip."

She chuckled softly. "No wonder your energy levels were depleted. You're the most active man I know. Any shortness of breath? Chest pains? Tingling sensations?"

He shook his head.

"Good." She gave him a bright smile. "Mind getting on the table for me?"

He suppressed his groan and moved to the end of the exam table.

"You know the drill," she said.

Normally Rhys wasn't a self-conscious man, but sitting in the exam room, waiting to hear that his heart wasn't going to self-destruct, he was suddenly shy as he unbuttoned his shirt to give her access to his chest.

"Let's see what's going on in there." The healer pressed the cold metal piece of her stethoscope to his chest and told him to breathe normally. She moved it around a few times before pulling back. "Okay. You can button your shirt."

He was silent as he put himself together. And then he waited as she read his recent EKG scans. She scribbled more notes and then closed the folder and smiled at him.

"So... will I live?" he asked, his tone light. He asked her the same question every time, and every visit he held his breath while he waited for her to answer.

"It appears so. Everything sounds the same, but that former healer was right. Your energy levels are a little lower than I prefer, but I don't think it's from your activity level. You haven't really changed how much exercise you get, but just the form in which you're getting it."

His stomach clenched as he waited for her to continue. A drop in energy level in witches was as problematic as a spike in white blood cell counts. "Does that mean more tests?"

"Just a couple of blood tests for precaution. In the meantime, I want to switch your heart medication. I think the current one might be causing the fatigue." She handed him a prescription. "The active ingredient is the same, but the healer who makes it has a gentler hand."

"Okay. Should I start it right away?" he asked.

"Yes. And pick up a couple more energy potions. One every other day for the next week so you can get back to normal levels. I want to see you back here in two weeks just to see how the new treatment is going."

"You got it."

"Excellent. Good seeing you again, Rhys. Have a great day." She smiled at him and shook his hand.

"Thanks, Healer Snow." He stood, grateful to be off the exam table, and followed her out the door. They walked in step down the hallway. The healer headed to the front desk and Rhys headed to the small onsite lab. Just as they reached his destination, the lab door swung open, and Hanna came striding out of the room and ran right into him.

"Whoa!" he said, chuckling as he held her upright. "What are you doing here?"

She glanced from him to Snow. The healer waved at Hanna but didn't stop, and in the next moment she disappeared around the corner that led to the administration counter.

"I was getting blood drawn for a new trial. What are *you* doing here?" There was an accusation in her tone that made Rhys frown.

"Checkup. Nothing serious." He smiled at her. "I need to give some blood. Wait for me?"

"I guess." She frowned up at him. "Are you sure it's just a checkup? You look pale."

He laughed. "I'm sure. Just a regular thing to check levels and adjust meds."

She stepped back and blinked. "You're on meds?" Her voice was high-pitched, and uncertainty flashed in her pretty gaze.

"Hanna, relax," he said gently. "It's just a preventative. Nothing serious. I swear."

"You should've told me," she said, staring at her feet.

He used two fingers to gently lift her chin. "I would've. I just didn't think about it. It's no big deal. I promise." He jerked his head toward the door. "Want to go back in with me while I give them a pint of blood?"

She glanced back at the lab and gave a tiny shudder. "Uh, no. How about I just meet you at your house later? I need to run some errands in town before I head back to Keating Hollow." She leaned in and gave him a peck on the lips. "Sorry," she whispered and then took a deep breath. "I was just surprised to see you here today."

"It's okay," he said, understanding perfectly. If he hadn't known that she participated in drug trials, he'd have freaked out a little to find her there, too. Healer Snow dealt with all the tough cases in town. If she was your healer, it was because no one else was talented enough to treat you. "I'm fine. You're fine. And tonight, we'll be fine together." He winked at her. "How do you feel about homemade ice cream?"

"Cappuccino flavor?" she asked.

"I'm sure I can manage that." He gave her one last kiss on her forehead. "Go on, gorgeous. Get your stuff done so we can relax tonight."

She pulled him into a hug, and as she held on tight, she said, "What did I do to deserve you?"

"You were just you." He tightened his hold on her and added, "Or maybe it was all those cookies you passed me in homeroom way back in freshman year."

"I passed those cookies to you every day for four years, Rhys," she corrected.

"Right, but by the end of freshman year I was already in love with you, so those later ones didn't count."

She glanced up at him. "Really? Why didn't you say anything?"

He shrugged. "Too much trauma for both of us I guess. You were the only person I had, and I didn't want to mess it up by being a horny teenager."

Her lips split into a wide smile, and she laughed. "Okay, point taken. But just so you know, I was already in love with you, too."

Rhys groaned, hating how much time they'd wasted. "Damn my teenage chivalry."

"You can say that again," she said with a snort. "Now go. I'll see you tonight."

He pictured her in his house, holding a glass of wine in her hand. She was gorgeous in every way. He leaned in and pressed one last kiss to her cheek. "Love you."

Her smile widened, and love shone in her eyes as she said the words he'd been waiting forever to hear from her lips. "Love you, too."

CHAPTER 16

*H*anna steered her small SUV up the winding road to Rhys's house. She was still berating herself about the way she'd overreacted to seeing him at the clinic in Eureka. Immediately when she'd run into him, her only thought was that he'd been hiding his illness... just like Charlotte had done with everyone she loved, except her immediate family. Hanna's heart rate had shot up, and she'd started to sweat, terrified that Rhys hadn't told her everything.

Of course he hadn't. She couldn't have known he was taking preventative care medication because he'd never talked about what could happen. She understood why, but she hoped he wasn't in denial, because no matter how much she hated to admit it, her mother was at least partially right. If Hanna was going to go all-in on this relationship with Rhys, she needed to accept that there was a real possibility she'd lose him prematurely. And she had to make peace with that.

Rhys's small house came into view, and Hanna turned into his driveway, parking right next to his Jeep. She climbed out of her vehicle and then went around to the passenger side to gather the items she'd picked up on her way over. By the time she started for the front door, Rhys was already standing on the porch, waiting for her.

"Hey," he said, casting a long, lingering glance down her body. She'd changed into a skirt and an off-the-shoulder blouse and had pinned her hair up, accentuating her long neck and her toned shoulders. In her opinion, they were her best feature. Rhys met her on his sidewalk and took the canvas grocery bag from her. "You do know I was in charge of dinner, right?"

She chuckled. "You know I can't go anywhere without bringing something."

He grabbed her hand and tugged her inside. It had been a while since she'd been to his house, but nothing had changed. The living room was still decorated with bachelor-style well-worn leather furniture, a couple of coastal prints, and a plain wood coffee table. It wasn't fit for a spread in *Better Homes and Gardens*, but she knew from experience that the couch was very comfortable.

"All right, gorgeous, what did you bring us?" Rhys asked as he placed the bag on his counter and started pulling the items out.

"A cabernet to go with your tri-tip, some special decaf roast to have with the ice cream, and coffee cake for breakfast," Hanna said, taking a seat across from him on one of his stools.

"Breakfast, huh?" He gave her a hopeful glance. "Will you be here to share it with me?"

She shrugged one shoulder, remaining noncommittal.

He chuckled. "Mysterious. I like that."

"Okay, what do you need help with?" She popped up off the stool and rounded the counter. "I'm starving."

"Just need to get the salads out of the fridge. I've got the rest," he said.

"I'm on it." Hanna moved to the stainless steel sub-zero refrigerator and felt a twinge of jealousy. Her own fridge was a hand-me-down from her parents. It was fine, but it wasn't nearly as pretty or efficient as his. Inside, she found two ready-to-eat salads and pulled them out, noting the goat cheese and walnuts—her favorite. "Yum, Rhys. You're already scoring points and I haven't even seen the main course yet."

"That's good news," he said through the window. He'd disappeared outside, no doubt checking on his grill. "Take them to the table. I'll be right in."

"Sure thing. Want me to open the wine?" she asked.

"Not yet. I've got something else I want you to try."

"Okay." She glanced at the small table and let out the tiniest gasp of surprise. It was gorgeous, set with cloth napkins, fresh-cut flowers, and a set of dinnerware she'd pointed out to Rhys months ago in a catalog. But the icing on the cake was the candelabra that illuminated the romantic scene.

She placed the salads down on the elegant blue and gold-rimmed plates and took a seat, waiting as the butterflies fluttered in her gut. Hanna had spent countless hours in this house, but never as Rhys's girlfriend. She wasn't quite sure how to act.

The sliding glass door opened, and Rhys strolled in with two plates, one full of tri-tip and the other grilled veggies. The scent of freshly grilled meat filled the air, making Hanna's stomach rumble.

"Everything looks wonderful," she said to him as he deposited the food onto the table.

"I hope it lives up to the hype." He grinned and headed back into the kitchen to pull a glass bottle out of the fridge. It had a rubber stopper and was the type of bottle he'd use for his cider making. Once he made it back to the table, he held the bottle up, revealing the gorgeous golden color. "Ready for a taste test?"

"Absolutely."

Rhys removed the stopper and filled two glasses. Then he took his seat and raised his glass. "To a new beginning for both of us."

Hanna raised her glass to his and said, "To a long future full of love, joy, and passion."

"Passion," he echoed and clinked his glass to hers. "Definitely."

"You would latch onto that one," she said, suddenly feeling shy.

"You're the one who brought it up." He reached across the table and squeezed her hand. "You're adorable when you're embarrassed, you know that?"

"I'm not embarrassed," she said, feeling like an idiot. Of course she was embarrassed. She'd just toasted to passion and they hadn't even spent the night together yet. And her nerves were all over the place, making her wonder if she could even relax enough to enjoy dinner.

"Try the cider, Hanna," he said, his eyes glinting with amusement.

Did he know what she was thinking? She wouldn't put it past him. He could usually read her thoughts so well she often wondered if he had a direct line to her brain.

"It'll help you relax, Han," he said gently. "Come on. It's just me. How many times have we sat at this table and had dinner together?"

She glanced at the gorgeous table and laughed a nervous chuckle. "Too many to count. But this is the first time you've ever lit candles or bought flowers."

He eyed the table. "I was trying to be romantic."

Gods, she was seriously messing this up. What was wrong

with her? "I know. And it's beautiful, Rhys. I appreciate the effort. I really do. It's just... I don't know, it feels like there's an expectation at the end of this meal, and now it's the only thing I can think about."

He put his glass down. "I don't expect anything. And I sure as heck don't expect you to fall into my bed on our second real date since last year. I just wanted you to know how special you are."

Gah! She knew that. Why was all of this such a big deal? It wasn't as if she'd never been with a man. She was in her late-twenties for goodness sake. It was just that she'd never been with *this* man. The one she'd been waiting for since she was a teenager. "I think I might be a little overwhelmed with the intensity of everything."

He watched her for a moment and then nodded his understanding. "Okay then. Change of scenery." He grabbed his salad plate and his glass of cider and got to his feet. "Come on. Grab your glass and your plate. We're moving to the couch."

"What?" She laughed even as she did as she was told and followed him into the living room.

He took his spot at the end of the couch and patted the cushion for her to curl up next to him. "Right here, love. Just like usual."

She giggled as she sank into the couch. "Usually we have Chinese takeout and a bad movie."

"We can try that next if this doesn't work out." He took a long swig of his cider and nodded for her to do the same.

Finally, the butterflies settled, and she tasted the cider. She closed her eyes and found the flavor profile to be fresh and crisp with notes of cherry. "Yum. Good gracious, Rhys. This is delicious."

"You think so?"

Her eyes popped open. And he way he was looking at her, his eyes full of heat, she had the feeling that he was thinking that she was the delicious one. But somehow, now that they were on his old couch, she didn't feel the strange pressure she felt before despite his obvious desire. She had no idea why she felt more comfortable on the couch, but she loved that Rhys had known exactly how to put her at ease. "I know so. I love it. Is this one you made for Lincoln Townsend?"

"Yep. I'm going to take him some samples later this week." He sat facing her and tucked a curl behind her ear. "Want to come with me when I go?"

"Yes," she said without hesitation. She loved the Townsends and Lincoln especially. It would give her a chance to check in on him, to see how he was doing now that he was done with his cancer treatments.

"Good. Now eat your salad so we can move onto the steak. I thought you were starving?"

"I was, but..." She shrugged and took a bite of her salad. Flavor exploded over her tongue. He'd used some sort of flavored vinaigrette; she just wasn't sure which. "Pomegranate?" she guessed.

"Almost," he said with a nod. "It's a combination of raspberry and pomegranate. It's good, right?"

"It's excellent." Hanna turned her attention from Rhys to her salad, and the next thing she knew, her plate was empty. If she'd had bread, she would've soaked up the remaining dressing.

"I guess you liked it," he said with a chuckle, taking her plate from her.

She pushed herself up off the couch and followed him to the table, but instead of taking the plate of tri-tip and veggies back to the couch, she sat at the table and waved for him to sit across from her. "I'm fine now, Rhys. Let's enjoy this beautiful table. We can go back to the couch for dessert."

He gave her a sexy half smile. "Sounds good to me."

❦

THE TRI-TIP HAD TURNED out to be the best meal Hanna had consumed since the last time she and Rhys had been together. The man was a real connoisseur of tender and delicious cuts of beef, and she'd missed his expertise. If left to her own devices, she'd normally just pass because that would mean cooking, something she didn't really have time to do anyway. Not if she wanted to get a few hours of sleep before heading to work at the crack of dawn.

"Dessert now, or do you want to head to town for a walk along the river?" Rhys asked.

Hanna eyed the empty cider bottle, the one she'd drained, and said, "Do you have more of that?"

Rhys chuckled. "Yes."

"Okay. Grab it, and let's head for the river. It's beautiful out tonight."

"You got it." Rhys disappeared into the kitchen for a moment and returned with a full bottle of cider and a couple of plastic cups.

Rhys, who'd only had the one glass of cider, drove them down the hill and parked his Jeep on Main Street. With the cider and two cups in hand, he led an already slightly tipsy Hanna along the town's special golf cart-only path that led to the river. The moon shone brightly overhead, and the night smelled of fresh dew and cut grass.

"This is really nice," Hanna said, clutching his arm and leaning into him. "Romantic. It's the perfect date, Rhys."

"It's always perfect with you around," he said.

Hanna snorted, completely amused by his statement. "That's pure cheese."

"Maybe. But it's the truth." He kissed the top of her head and continued along the path.

Her heart melted just a little, and she decided that she was good with cheese. In fact, she was all-in on the concept.

"Hanna? Rhys? Is that you?" a voice called from down by the bank of the river.

Hanna pulled away from Rhys and squinted. Down by the shoreline she could just make out the outline of a golf cart. "Wanda? Is that you?"

"Yep. Get down here. The hot spring is fantastic." Wanda was Abby's golf cart-racing buddy and if there were shenanigans going on in Keating Hollow, Wanda was usually at the center. Fun was Wanda's religion. She and Abby had a friendly rivalry with the golf cart races and last Hanna heard, Abby was winning the race count by double digits.

She glanced up at Rhys. "I suppose we should go say hi?"

"Sure. If you want to," he said, already angling for the shore.

Hanna wasn't all that interested in visiting, actually. She'd been enjoying her time alone with Rhys and wanted to keep him to herself, but it would be rude to ignore them.

As they moved closer, laughter filtered through the night air, the sound tinkling off the river. And when they crested the gently rolling riverbank, Hanna spotted the second golf cart. Judging from the mud plastered on the side of Abby Townsend's cart, it was safe to say they'd already raced for the evening.

"Hanna!" Abby called from the water. Faith, Wanda, Brian, Shannon, and the new girl Luna were all with her in the natural spring that was adjacent to the river. "Get over here."

After kicking off her shoes, Hanna moved to the edge of the river and peered at them. "Who won this round?"

Abby groaned as Wanda sat up in the water and pointed both of her index fingers in her own direction. "My team kicked her lily-white ass. I'm back in the game, baby!"

"We helped," Brian said with a roll of his eyes. "Without those fire dragons dancing across the river, Abby never would've been distracted enough to hit that giant mud puddle Faith caused with her ill-advised water nymph she had trouble controlling."

The golf cart races were rife with magic obstacles. The rules were there really weren't any rules, and the drivers often chose their running mates based on what magical talents they had.

"Dancing fire dragons?" Hanna asked. "I'd really like to see that."

"Then get your pretty ass in here, and I'll recreate the show for you."

Rhys cleared his throat. "Are you flirting with my girl, Brian?"

"Me?" the man asked innocently. "Never."

"Sure, Bri," Shannon, the woman who ran Miss Maple's chocolate shop, chimed in with a snort. "Whatever you say."

Brian was somewhat new in town. He was best friends with Jacob, Yvette Townsend's fiancé, and had moved to Keating Hollow about a year ago. He'd taken Faith out a few times before she settled with Hunter. Hanna wondered who he might end up with. It appeared he was currently keeping his options open with Shannon on one side of him and Luna on the other.

"Hi Luna," Hanna said. "How's it going at the spa?"

"Great," she said almost shyly as she sunk a little lower in the spring. "Faith has been wonderful, and I really enjoy working there."

"That's good." She smiled at the woman.

"Are you two going to get in here or what?" Wanda asked. "It's glorious. Especially if you need to recharge."

Hanna looked at Rhys. "What do you say?"

He shrugged. "We didn't bring suits."

Faith let out a loud whistle. "Who needs suits? Just strip down to your underwear. That's what we did."

Hanna felt her face flush. "I'm going to need more cider."

Rhys chuckled and filled a glass for her. "Here."

"Thanks." Hanna downed it and asked for a refill.

He leaned in close. "We don't have to do this if you're uncomfortable."

She shook her head. "No. I want to." Her foot slipped slightly in the grass, making her stumble.

Rhys caught her and chuckled. "Whoa there. You all right?"

"Yep." Hanna felt wonderful all over, and the idea of cozying up to Rhys in the water was entirely too tempting. Smiling at him, she handed him her cup, discarded her skirt, and tugged her shirt over her head.

Rhys's eyes nearly bugged out of his head as he stared at her.

Hanna held his gaze for a moment. Then she laughed and ran into the spring. The water was glorious. It was warm, but not too hot, and buoyant enough that she could just float even in the areas that were too deep for her feet to touch the bottom.

The gorgeous man she'd left on the riverbank tracked her with his eyes until she lifted a finger and beckoned him. Rhys didn't hesitate. He pulled his shirt and pants off, but before he could plunge into the spring, Hanna called, "Bring the cider!"

Always one to please, Rhys filled both cups and waded in. He passed one to her and sent the other one around for everyone else to taste.

Murmurs of approval went around the group, and soon the bottle was empty.

"Luna," Hanna slurred slightly. Her vision was starting to get a little fuzzy. Oops. She might have imbibed just a little too much. She swallowed and tried to focus on the newcomer. "Tell us about yourself. Where are you from?"

Luna glanced down at the water as she said, "I'm from the bay area, just north of San Francisco."

"Oh? Marin county?"

Luna bobbed her head.

"It's gorgeous there," Hanna said, squinting to make out her features. But the other woman was just a blur. When Hanna spoke again, her voice was too loud, but she seemed unable to control herself. "I did a photoshoot out in Point Reyes once. I just love the coast, don't you?"

"It was okay."

"Are your parents still down there?" Faith asked, moving over to sit next to Luna.

The other woman shook her head. "No. I grew up in foster care. I left as soon as I turned eighteen."

That was a conversation stopper. Hanna reached out and tried to pat her on the shoulder, but Luna twisted in the water at that exact moment, and Hanna accidentally ended up clocking her in the face.

"Ouch!" Luna cried.

"Ohmigod! I'm so sorry." Hanna inched closer, wanting to take a look at the damage, but she couldn't clear her vision and she was having trouble holding her head up. She felt herself sinking in the water and as she took a breath, she sucked in a mouthful of spring water. Her lungs seized, and she started coughing uncontrollably, trying to dispel the liquid. Her eyes watered, and she heard people talking around her, but her vision was turning black at the edges. The stars above had turned into glaring lights, and suddenly she started to panic.

"Rhys! Rhys!" she sputtered.

"I've got you, Hanna," his soothing voice said in her ear. "You're okay."

She felt his strong arms around her and the cool sting of the night air. She blinked up at him, not at all sure what had happened. But the world was spinning, and her stomach rolled.

"Let's get you home, okay?" he said.

"Okay." She closed her eyes and prayed she wouldn't vomit on him.

CHAPTER 17

*R*hys stared down at Hanna's peaceful face, his heart full of love. After the cider caught up with her the night before, he'd brought her back to his place, put her in one of his oversized T-shirts, and tucked her into his bed. He'd been torn as to whether he should leave her and sleep in the guestroom or stay to keep an eye on her. She'd been semicoherent while in his Jeep on the way home, but afterward she'd slipped in and out of consciousness. In the end, he decided he'd never get to sleep if he was worrying about her from the other side of the house.

So he'd pulled on sweat pants, crawled into bed beside her, and held her close enough that he could hear her deep breathing in his ear. Then he'd promptly fell asleep and slept better than he had in years.

The morning light filtered in through the window and shone on Hanna's face. Rhys propped himself up on one elbow and brushed her tousled curls out of her eyes.

She murmured something and rolled toward him, her hand curling at his chest as her eyes fluttered open.

"Hi," he said softly.

Her lips curled into a tiny smile. But then she frowned and suddenly jerked back and glanced around. "Um, Rhys?"

"Yeah, gorgeous?" He couldn't help but be amused by her morning-after confusion.

"What am I doing in your bedroom?" She lifted the covers and glanced down at herself in his T-shirt.

"You were sleeping it off. Too much cider." He dropped a kiss on her forehead. "Apparently, the combination of the hot springs and the cider got to you, and I had to put you to bed. I considered taking you home, but your car is here. Plus, I didn't want to dig around in your bag for your house key, so I brought you here and kept an eye on you."

"That's all you kept on me?" She scanned his body, her eyes lingering on his bare chest.

Damn, he thought. He'd dreamed of waking up next to her for years, only his version wasn't quite so PG. "I confess, I did hold you. I hope you don't mind too terribly."

She bit down on her bottom lip and glanced away. "No, I don't mind." Her face was pinched with embarrassment when she glanced back up at him. "I'm sorry, Rhys. Geez. I didn't mean to behave like a clueless teenager. Did I really have that much to drink?"

He shrugged one shoulder. "I didn't think you had *quite* that much. The alcohol content in the cider isn't any higher than the beers we serve at the brewery."

Hanna pushed herself up and frowned. "Hmm. I shouldn't have gotten that drunk, especially since I ate dinner."

"How do you feel this morning?" Rhys asked, peering at her. "Hungover at all?"

Hanna shook her head. "Nope. In fact, I feel pretty good." She smiled at him. "I guess you took good care of me."

"And I always will, love." He slid out of bed and pulled a T-shirt over his head. "Now, don't you have to work?"

Hanna glanced at the clock and groaned. "Why can't it be my day off?"

"Go on. Grab a shower. I'll make you breakfast."

She glanced at the en-suite bathroom and then back at him as if torn. He knew the feeling. The urge to climb back into bed with her was almost overwhelming. But now wasn't the time. When they finally took that step in their relationship, it wasn't going to be rushed. He was going to savor every inch of her.

"I'll get the coffee on," he said and then forced himself to head downstairs.

RHYS STOOD IN HIS DOORWAY, watching as Hanna steered her car down the road. He waited until her RAV4 disappeared around the bend, and then he shut the door and went back into his impossibly quiet house. It was strange how one night with her in his space suddenly made him question how he'd been content to live alone for so long. The idea that she wouldn't be there when he got off work that night made him actually feel a little lonely. And that rankled.

He had to get himself under control. Get back to some sort of normalcy. He should book a hang gliding session or head out to the airport. But he didn't have time for either, so instead he changed into his running clothes and took off into the woods. The cool air and light fog made it the perfect morning for a run. The pounding of his footsteps on the earth were a drumbeat that normally soothed and settled him. But that didn't happen, no matter how hard he tried to focus.

All Rhys could think about was Hanna and finally making her his once and for all. He pictured her in white, standing next to him, promising herself to him forever. The scene in his mind shifted to Hanna holding a little one swaddled in a soft pink blanket, both of his girls smiling up at him. First words, first steps, first day of school, it was all there running through his mind.

By the time he racked up seven miles and found himself back in his yard, he had a plan. But he needed a little help.

After a quick shower and another coffee to go, Rhys jumped in his Jeep and headed to A Touch of Magic.

The door to Faith's spa was still locked when Rhys arrived, but he could see Lena sitting behind the reception desk, and he winced. They'd dated for a short time not too long ago, but when she started pushing for more, he'd ended it. It wasn't fair to lead her on when he'd been fully aware that he was in love with someone else.

Rhys couldn't remember a time when he hadn't been in love with his best friend. Sure, he'd dated some in college when he was certain nothing would or could come of a relationship with Hanna, but he'd never felt the intoxicating mixture of love, desire, and pure friendship with any of those other women. That was reserved for Hanna. It always had been, and it always would be as far as he was concerned. He was sorry he'd hurt Lena, but it would've hurt far more to let her think they had a chance.

"Lena?" he called as he knocked on the glass door. He knew she'd heard him because her head popped up and she looked right at him. Only instead of coming to the door, she put her head down and continued to do something on the computer. "Lena?" he tried again. "I'm looking for Faith. Is she here?"

The receptionist stopped typing for a moment, but still she didn't look up. Her fingers started flying over the keys again as she continued to ignore him.

"Dammit, Lena," he muttered and pulled out his phone, scrolling for Faith's number. When he realized he didn't have it, he called the phone number displayed on the door.

"A Touch of Magic day spa, this is Lena. How may I help you?"

"Is Faith in? I need to talk to her," Rhys said into the phone.

"Oh. It's you." Her head popped up and she stared right at him. "Did you need an appointment?"

"No. I need to talk to Faith. Is she here?" he tried again.

"No." The line went dead, and Rhys scowled.

"Good morning," a soft voice said from behind him.

He spun and spotted Luna carrying a tray of coffees from Incantation Café. The pretty honey-blonde smiled kindly at him, her green eyes soft and welcoming.

"Do you have an early appointment?" she asked, knocking on the door.

"No. I'm looking for Faith," he said.

"Ahh, she's still at the café. She stopped in to check on Hanna. After last night she wanted to make sure she wasn't feeling too bad."

"Right," Rhys said, wondering if he should head to the café. But if he did, Hanna would want to know why he needed to talk to Faith. No. He'd wait at the spa. "She told me she was feeling fine."

"Lucky. The last time I was that drunk, I puked for days." She laughed, and the tinkling sound reminded him of Faith. Perhaps they were picking up on each other's norms now that they worked together.

"I think it was the combination of the hot springs and the cider. She's fine now," Rhys said, just as much to assure himself as to assure her.

"That's a possibility," Luna said with a nod.

The sound of a lock clicking caught Rhys's attention. He glanced over just in time to see Lena retreating from the door.

"Come on in and wait for her. I'm sure she'll be here any moment," Luna said.

Rhys eyed Lena's scowl and almost chickened out. But if he was going to follow through with his plan, it was going to take a fair bit of bravery. There was no better time to man up than the present. "Thanks."

He followed her into the elegant spa. The scent of vanilla permeated the air and instantly relaxed him. "This place is fantastic."

Lena let out a snort and turned her back to them.

"Something wrong?" Luna asked her.

"Nope. Just not interested in entertaining someone who can't even wait forty-five minutes until we open," she said and flipped her long dark hair over her shoulder.

Luna glanced between Rhys and Lena, a puzzled look on her face.

He leaned in and whispered, "We used to date. I called it off over the holidays."

"I see," she whispered back. "That's gotta sting."

Rhys just shrugged one shoulder. They hadn't even dated that long. It was hard for him to understand why Lena was so upset about it not working out.

His ex glared at him, and then with her hands balled into fists, she stormed out of the reception area into the back.

"That's messy," Luna said.

"You can say that again." Rhys frowned. "It's been almost three months. She can't still be mad, can she?"

Luna chuckled. "Oh, Rhys. You're such a man."

"What's that mean? Do you have some insight to share?" He was more curious than anything else.

"You just started things back up with Hanna, right?"

He nodded.

"Well, there you go. As long as you were single, she could either hold out hope that things would work out between you, or she could comfort herself with the fact that you just didn't want to be in a relationship. Neither of those things are true now. Her ego has taken a bit of a hit."

Rhys gaped at her. "Really? That seems like a lot of mental gymnastics."

"Welcome to the female brain." She patted his chest. "Come on. I'll take you to Faith's office."

Rhys followed her through the dimly lighted hallway until they got to the door all the way at the end of the hall.

"This is it." She opened the door and flicked the light on. The space was homey with an overstuffed couch on one wall and a couple of matching arm chairs directly across from it. In the back of the room there was a banker's desk that was full of pictures of her family, Hunter, and Zoey.

"Thanks. I appreciate this," Rhys said. "I need some advice about Hanna, and I really didn't want to ask in front of Lena."

"Completely understandable." She started to leave but then paused. "Faith and Hanna are best friends, right?"

"Yeah. They're really close. Like sisters," Rhys said with a nod as he sank into Faith's couch. "They've known each other their whole lives."

Luna sighed wistfully. "I've always wondered what it would be like to have a sister, to have that closeness. I've mostly been on my own, you know?"

"Well wonder no longer, Luna-girl," Faith said as she strode into the room. "'Cause we're family now. And you're stuck with me."

Luna's entire face lit up with her smile. "You're too nice to me, Faith."

"Not nice enough, I'm afraid. Not if you don't realize I've

already got my claws into you." She winked at Luna. "Seriously, you're great, and I couldn't be happier to have you here both personally and professionally."

"Thanks, Faith," Luna said shyly. "I really like it here, too."

"Good." Faith returned the woman's smile and then turned her attention to Rhys. "Have you had a chance to let this magical creature work on your back yet?"

Rhys shook his head. "No, in fact I haven't been able to get an appointment for a couple of weeks now. You're always full."

"What?" Faith frowned and picked up the phone. "Lena? Yeah. I need you to put Rhys on the books for some time this week. No, I don't care if we're booked. Make it before we open if you have to." There was a pause. Then she barked, "And don't ever turn him away again. Figure something out or ask me. He's been one of my best clients since we opened." She tossed the phone back onto its cradle and shook her head, clearly irritated. When she glanced back up, she was all smiles. "Day after tomorrow at nine. Does that work?"

"Hell, yes," he said. "Thanks."

"I'm going to go get the rooms ready," Luna said. "It was nice talking to you, Rhys."

"You, too." He waved as she disappeared into the hall.

"All right," Faith said, taking a seat in one of the armchairs. "What are you here for? To complain about Lena?"

Rhys laughed. "No. But she does seem to hate me quite a bit."

"She'll get over it." Faith leaned forward and clasped her hands together. "So?"

"I need your help." Rhys's gut clenched with nerves. "Do you have any time today or tomorrow to head over to Vallente's?"

"Vallente's? Why would you... Oh! Oh my god!" She popped

out of the chair and let out a gasp as she added, "Rhys, you're not… I mean, you are, aren't you?"

"I am. It's been long enough." Her excitement had him grinning. This was the right thing to do. He was sure of it.

"I'll make time. Let's see." She ran over to her computer and scanned her schedule. She bit on her lower lip, contemplating. Then her eyes lit up and she grabbed the phone. After punching in a number, she said, "Abby? I need to move your appointment. I know, but it's important. Trust me, when you learn why, you're going to be thrilled." She fiddled with a pen, bobbing her head up and down. "Yes, it's that good. Okay, just come by after hours. I'll stay late." Faith gave Rhys a thumbs-up. "See you then. Love you!" The phone rattled as she dropped it back in place.

"You didn't have to cancel an appointment that makes you work late," Rhys said, feeling guilty for messing with her schedule.

"Oh, yes, I did. I'm free at eleven. Meet me there?"

"You got it." Excitement and nerves mixed together, making him antsy. And then nauseated. If he was going to do this, he needed to talk to Hanna's parents. He glanced at the clock. He had two hours. And it was time to face the music.

CHAPTER 18

*R*hys stood on the front porch of the Pelsh residence, feeling as if he was going to puke. He knew what they'd be thinking, hell he'd be thinking it himself. They'd only dated for a few months just over a year ago, and now they'd been back together for all of five minutes. This wasn't going to go well, but he was going to do it anyway.

Sucking in a deep fortifying breath, he knocked on the door.

It opened almost immediately. "It's about time you decided to knock," Mary Pelsh said, not bothering to hide her displeasure. "I thought you were just going to pace the porch all morning."

"Good morning, Mrs. Pelsh," he said, ignoring her outburst. "I was hoping I could talk to you and Mr. Pelsh for a few minutes."

"Walter!" Mary called. "The boy you and Hanna like so much is here."

The boy. Now that was funny. Last he checked he was pushing thirty.

"Rhys? Is that you?" he heard Walter Pelsh call out. "It's about time you came to visit me." Mr. Pelsh appeared in the doorway, the sunshine bouncing off his shaved head. He tugged Rhys into the house and asked, "What have you been up to, my friend?"

"The usual. Working at the brewery, hiking, hang gliding. Nothing too crazy."

Walter let out a bark of laughter. "Hanna tells me you got your pilot's license. I'd say that's a little crazy."

Mrs. Pelsh let out a snort of disapproval as she followed them, and Rhys winced.

"Now, now, Mary," Walter said, gently admonishing her. "The boy's just living his life. There's nothing wrong with that."

"There is if he's reckless and hurts Hanna," she said.

Rhys wasn't sure how to handle that statement. He was careful in everything he did. Responsible, curious, and above all, he respected the dangers of the extreme sports he participated in. Not that he'd call flying planes extreme. But he could see how she might get that idea.

"What's reckless about flying?" Walter asked, his tone non-confrontational. "You've flown before, Mary. In fact, we even flew in one of those private jets over to Tahoe that one year. Remember that?" He turned to Rhys. "I had a buddy up in Trinidad who decided to elope to Tahoe and flew us all over at the last minute. Boy was that ever a hoot."

"Yeah, a real hoot. You were green for two days after the turbulence," Mary said, striding into the kitchen. She fiddled with the tea pot, and Rhys understood it was just a way to keep her hands busy. She was an air witch with a special talent for telekinesis. If she wanted tea made, all she had to do was wave a hand and the rest would take care of itself.

"We can't all have guts of steel, now can we?" Walter took a seat at the table and pulled a tray of croissants toward him. "Sit. Have a little brunch while we catch up."

Rhys did as he was told but passed on the croissants. He was too nervous. It wasn't every day you asked for a woman's hand in marriage.

"Tell me what you've been up to, Mr. Pelsh," Rhys said. "I haven't seen you around the café lately."

"That's because I'm retired," he said, puffing his chest out as if he'd conquered the impossible.

"You don't act retired," Mary muttered under her breath.

That got another chuckle out of Walter. He leaned closer to Rhys. "I've been working on cultivating a vineyard."

"Winery?" Rhys asked with one eyebrow raised.

"Yep. I've had a small vineyard for years just as a hobby, but now that Hanna has partnered at the café, I have time to follow my passions. I'll be bottling my first wines this fall."

"Wow. That's incredible. Congratulations," Rhys said, thrilled for the man. "Very exciting."

"Yes, it is." He nodded to his wife as she set a carafe of hot water, two teacups, and a variety of loose leaf teas in front of them. "Thanks, honey. We appreciate it."

"Yes, Mrs. Pelsh. The teas look wonderful."

"You're welcome," she said with what sounded like a defeated sigh. Then she grabbed a cup for herself and the cream and sugar before she joined them.

Mr. Pelsh chose the acai green tea and set it to seep.

Rhys followed his lead and said, "I'd love to help in any way I can with the winery. I've been having some success with ciders over at the brew pub. Lincoln Townsend asked me to make up some batches and if all goes well, they'll be moving into that market, soon."

"Wonderful!" Mr. Pelsh glanced at his wife. "I told you this one was going places."

"Yeah, he's going to walk right out of Hanna's life again," she said, keeping her eyes on Rhys. "And then we'll be stuck picking up the pieces."

"Mary. Stop that nonsense. Hanna and Rhys's relationship is for them to figure out. Not you. Stop sabotaging." Walter was angry now, and it took Rhys aback. He couldn't remember ever witnessing a fight between Hanna's parents. And he wasn't at all pleased they were fighting over him.

"Excuse me, Mr. Pelsh," Rhys said. "I think Mrs. Pelsh has every right to be skeptical of me. I fully admit that in the past, I have been reluctant to commit to Hanna. But believe me, it had nothing to do with how much I love her." He sat back in the chair, really hearing his words for the first time. "Actually, scratch that. It probably has everything to do with how much I love her."

"I always knew you cared deeply for her, son," Mr. Pelsh said.

"If you love her so much, you'll stop hurting her, Rhys," Mary said quietly.

"I think I should explain." Rhys took a long sip of his tea, hoping it would fortify him. Unfortunately, there was no such luck. "See, I carry the gene that caused my father's and my grandfather's premature deaths. I have fully expected to not live to be over the age of forty."

"That explains the extreme sports," Walter said with an understanding smile.

Rhys chuckled. "Yes… and no. Did you know that when Hanna was in high school, she's the one who brought up wanting to learn to fly?"

"No, she didn't. My daughter never—" Mary started.

"Yes, she did," Walter said, cutting her off. "About a month after we lost Charlotte. Don't you remember when she started badgering me for lessons?"

Mary blinked at him. "She did?"

"Yes. And you were not having it. That's why she tried out for the surfing team," he said.

"I didn't want her to do that either," Mary said into her teacup.

"It was a hard time, sweetheart. Don't beat yourself up about it."

Rhys started to feel like an intruder on their decade-old pain and wondered if he should excuse himself.

"That's why I told Rhys to do it with her. So he could keep an eye on her," Walter added and patted the younger man's arm. "And he did. She never once got hurt out there in the Pacific."

Rhys gave the older man a nod. "I have to admit we both loved it. It was the one place where nothing else touched us." He meant the pain of losing the people they loved, but it had also been an outlet for his confusing teenage emotions.

"We all know that grief takes time, son," Walter said. "Everyone deals with it in their own way. I suppose surfing under the direction of a coach was better than a sixteen-year-old learning to fly."

Rhys laughed. "I guess so."

Mary cleared her throat. "What does surfing have to do with your relationship with Hanna now, Rhys? What changed your mind, and why should we be happy that you've suddenly decided that it's okay to let Hanna walk your uncertain journey with you?"

"Mary," Walter said very quietly. "You're not saying what I think you're saying, are you?"

"I'm sure I am, Walter. Someone needs to look out for Hanna's well-being. What do you think it's going to do to her when she finds herself with two babies and no husband five years from now?" She gave Rhys a pained looked. "I'm not trying to be cruel, Rhys. I'm not." Tears filled her dark eyes. "You've been a huge part of our lives, too, you know. No one wants you to leave us prematurely. But there's no ignoring that it's a great risk. And our girl has been through so much all ready." She squeezed her eyes shut and shook her head. "I don't know if I can watch her suffer like that again."

Rhys didn't know if she meant the pain Hanna had been in after they lost Charlotte or if she was talking about the last time Rhys had called things off. It seemed pretty over-the-top if she was referring to the breakup. But he hadn't exactly been there for Hanna, had he? He knew he'd pissed her off, but he didn't know he'd broken her heart. Clueless. That's what he was. Completely clueless.

It was Rhys's turn to suck in a deep breath. He let it out slowly and got right to the point. "Listen, I don't know what's going to happen next week, next month, or next year. I can tell you that I spend a lot of time with a healer getting checked out, taking preventative medications, and taking care of myself in general. I've spent my entire adult life trying to protect Hanna from what might happen. But then I learned that she also carries a gene that could drastically alter her life."

"Nothing is going to happen to Hanna," Mary Pelsh said stubbornly.

Walter turned to her, squeezed her hand gently, and said, "We are hopeful that it doesn't. The odds are good that what happened with Charlotte won't affect her, but we don't know that for sure, love."

Mary pulled her hand away from her husband. "I don't want to talk about that."

"Fair enough. It's not my favorite topic either," Rhys said. "But it made me realize that Hanna is fearless. She doesn't sit around worrying about what-ifs. She lives without regret. It's courageous and inspiring, and I'm taking her lead. If she can be brave, then so can I."

"Good for you, son. So, when are you going to ask her?" Walter asked him with a gleam in his eye.

Mary sucked in a sharp breath. "Ask her what?"

Rhys's palms were sweaty, and his heart was a little erratic, but he steeled himself and prepared to have Mary Pelsh throw him out. "Mr. and Mrs. Pelsh, I'm planning to ask Hanna to marry me tomorrow. I'd like to first ask you for your blessing."

"Of course, Rhys," Walter said automatically. "Now that you've removed your head from your backside, I'd be honored to have you as a son-in-law."

"No!" Mrs. Pelsh cried. "It's irresponsible. You can't do this to her."

"Mary!" Walter stood and loomed over her, his expression full of disappointment. "You can't make this decision for Hanna. It's her life. You have to let her live it as she sees fit."

"She's not thinking clearly," his wife said, but her voice was soft and a little shaky.

"I'm pretty sure it's *you* who isn't thinking clearly." Walter crossed his arms over his chest. "You just dismissed a man based on a genetic abnormality that he can't control any more than Charlotte could control hers. What would you have said to her if she'd just stopped living... stopped loving... because she was afraid for her or Drew's future?"

"Charlotte was a teenager—" Mary started.

"She knew what was coming," Walter said quietly, his voice strained with the decade-old loss. "We all did. And yet, did anyone warn Drew?"

"No," she said, staring into her tea.

"He survived it, didn't he? Would you have deprived either Charlotte or Drew their time together because of the inevitable?"

"No." She slammed her eyes shut.

"Then I hope you can find it within yourself to accept whatever Hanna's answer is tomorrow, and I also suggest that you apologize to Rhys. He does not deserve to be treated like a ghost of a person." Walter wasn't shy about letting his frustration show, but there was plenty of understanding in his soft tone, too. The older man turned to Rhys. "You're a good man, and I'd be honored to call you son-in-law." He held his hand out.

Rhys felt a warm tightening in his chest as he shook the man's hand. "Thank you, sir."

Mary Pelsh got to her feet, opened her mouth, but then slammed it closed and ran out of the room. Her footsteps were heard on the stairs shortly before a bedroom door slammed.

Walter sighed. "She'll come around eventually. I think this has more to do with her lingering grief over Charlotte than it does you."

"I wish there was something I could do to ease her concerns," Rhys said.

"Me, too, son. Me, too."

CHAPTER 19

*R*hys tapped his fingers rapidly against the Jeep's steering wheel. He'd only gotten four hours of sleep the night before and was running on pure adrenaline and too much caffeine. He rarely had more than one cup in the morning, but he'd needed liquid courage, and alcohol was out of the question. Coffee had stepped in, but now he was paying for it. His nerves were off-the-charts jumpy.

But then Hanna's small house came into view, and he spotted her sitting on her porch swing. She was dressed in leggings, a sweat shirt, and her hiking boots, looking like his fantasy come true. He loved that she was just as excited as he was to hike ten miles to the top of a clearing, not only for the view but because she enjoyed the challenge, just like he did.

Rhys parked the Jeep right behind her RAV4 and jumped out. "Looks like you're more than ready to go."

"I was ready a half hour ago," she said, leaning in to give him a soft kiss on the lips.

"You mean I had that third cup of coffee for no reason?"

"Oh, Rhys. You didn't." Her pretty lips curved down in disapproval. "You're going to be a jittery mess all day."

"Nah. I'm fine," he lied. She was right of course. Keeping his leg still on the ride over had proved impossible. But who could blame him? Today could be the biggest day of his life. "Come here." He pulled her into a hug, wrapping his arms around her just because he could.

"Your heart is thundering away in there," she said, pressing her palm to his chest. "You better hydrate." She rummaged around in her backpack she'd had slung over one shoulder, producing a banana. "And eat this. It should help."

He grinned at her stupidly. God, he prayed she'd say yes. He loved how adorable she was when she was bossing him around.

"Why are you looking at me like that?" She frowned.

"I love you."

Her irritation melted away, and her expression softened as she said, "I love you, too. Now eat the banana so you don't have a potassium crisis."

"Yes, ma'am." He took the piece of fruit she offered and tugged her over to the Jeep. "Let's get out of here."

"Finally," she said with mock irritation as she jumped into the passenger seat while he took his place behind the wheel. "I've been dying to get out for weeks now. Where are we headed? Did you say?"

"Witchling Peak. On the way back, I thought we'd stop at the pools."

"Perfect. And this time, I won't even pass out on you." She grinned. "Unless you stashed some cider in a cooler I don't know about."

"Definitely not. Just water today." That was a lie, too. He had a small bottle of champagne in his backpack, but that would only surface after she said yes.

Even though the trail entrance wasn't that far away, it still took over an hour to get there due to the winding mountain roads. But because it was a weekday and the trail was somewhat out of the way, Rhys's Jeep was the only vehicle in the small parking area.

"Looks like we have the place to ourselves today," Rhys said.

"Perfect," Hanna said, taking the lead.

The hike was nothing short of magical. The forest was alive with pink, purple, white, and yellow wildflowers that thrived beneath the canopy of the majestic redwoods. They wound their way along a stream, around a giant redwood that had split the path, and paused at the crystal clear pools that reminded Rhys of what one would normally find in a tropical forest. "Do you want to pause for a dip now or when we're on our way back down?" Rhys asked her.

Hanna bent and trailed her fingers through the cold water. "It's a good thing we have the ability to heat this pond, otherwise we'd freeze our butts off."

Rhys chuckled. "No polar bear club for you?"

"No way." She shook her head and gave him a look that said he was slightly crazy. "I'm not into freezing my bits off."

"I have other plans for those bits," he said, his voice coming out husky and full of heat.

She stood and walked over to him, placing her hand on his shoulder. Her touch was warm even through his T-shirt, and it was all he could do to not tug her down onto the forest floor and show her exactly how much he wanted her.

"We better wait until we come back down from the peak, otherwise I have a feeling we might not make it up there at all."

There was so much desire in her heated gaze that Rhys actually groaned. "Hanna. Gods."

She laughed. "Suck it up, Silver. We have a hike to finish. Think of the dip in the pools as your reward."

"You're going to be my reward, gorgeous." He tugged on her hand. "Let's go. I don't want to wait any longer than we have to."

The last third of the hike was steeper and more treacherous than Rhys remembered, but Hanna handled it like a champ. Damn, she was in good shape. In fact, Rhys was the one having trouble catching his breath, and by the time they made it to the peak, he was breathing hard and needed a moment to get himself together. He sat on the stone that overlooked the Keating Hollow valley and waited for his pulse to slow.

Hanna sat down next to him and pulled out her camera. "Goddess above, Rhys," she whispered. "This place is gorgeous."

"Not as gorgeous as you," he said, still a little short of breath.

She glanced over at him and grinned. "Someone has been slacking on the incline portion of his workout."

He nodded his agreement. "Apparently so. Maybe we should start working out together." He patted her knee. "Clearly, you've got that part covered."

"When?" She laughed. "With our schedules, it would have to be either at midnight or four in the morning."

Rhys grimaced because she wasn't wrong. He turned to watch her profile and said, "It might be easier to find time if we lived together."

Her eyes widened with surprise as she turned to him. "Um, Rhys, is this your way of asking me to move in with you?"

"How would you feel about that?" he asked and nearly kicked himself. That wasn't at all what he'd intended to say. She opened her mouth, but he held a hand up. "No, don't answer that."

"Why?" Her face was a mix of disappointment and confusion.

"Because, Hanna, my love. I have an entirely different question I want to ask you." He reached into his pocket and pulled out the vintage rose gold, oval diamond ring Faith had helped him choose and held it out to her.

"Rhys?" Hanna asked, her voice shaking. "What are you doing?"

All of his nerves fled, and an eerie calm came over him as he smiled gently at her. "Hanna, you have been my best friend for so many years. Then you weren't, and it was devastating, I think for both of us. But now we've found our way back to each other, and I just don't want to waste any more time. I love you. I always have. Will you do me the honor of being my wife? Will you marry me?"

CHAPTER 20

*H*anna couldn't move as she stared at that beautiful ring in Rhys's hand. She'd heard what he'd said, felt his words deep in her bones. Her heart was nearly bursting from joy. This is what she'd always wanted. Rhys had just asked her to marry him. She should be screaming yes. Jumping up in excitement. Throwing her arms around him. Crying the happiest tears.

Instead she heard her mother's words in the back of her mind. *It is unreasonable for a man to take a wife knowing his heart is on borrowed time.* Panic set in and tears sprang to her eyes. One single tear rolled down her cheek. She stood and shook her head as she backed away, hating herself for her reaction. "I'm sorry, Rhys, I..."

"Hanna? What's wrong?" Rhys jumped up and took a step forward, but even as he was reaching for her with one hand, he clutched his chest with the other and sucked in a sharp breath.

"Rhys! Oh my god. Are you okay?" Hanna cried. "What's wrong?"

He blinked at her and opened his mouth to say something,

but then the color drained from his face, turning him a sickly shade of gray as he fell to the ground.

"Rhys!" Hanna dropped to her knees, pressing her fingers to his pulse. It took her a moment to locate it, but it was there. A little thready, but definitely there. "Thank the gods!" Leaning down, she put her ear near his mouth. Yes, he was breathing. A tiny wave of relief rushed through her. He'd just passed out. "Rhys?" she tried again. "Wake up. Come on, baby. We're on top of this mountain, and you can't do this to me. You just asked me to marry you. You have to wake up so I can say yes."

His eyelids fluttered, but he didn't open his eyes.

She wanted to sob. The urge to just completely break down and give in to her overwhelming emotions was right at the surface, but she couldn't do that. Rhys was counting on her. She quickly rummaged through her backpack and grabbed her phone. It was a longshot that she'd have service on the mountain, but she had to try. After getting to her feet, she held the phone up high, looking for bars. There weren't any.

"Dammit!" She ran across the clearing, tears making her eyes blurry. If she didn't find reception, she was going to have to haul him out of there in a fireman's carry. She was strong and knew she could do it; she just didn't know if she had the stamina to do it for miles until they got back to his car.

The phone suddenly beeped indicating she had a message. "Oh, thank the heavens." She immediately dialed 911.

"911, what's your emergency?"

"I'm on a hike at Witchling Peak and my fiancé just collapsed at the summit. He was clutching his heart."

"Is he breathing?"

"Yes." Hanna glanced over at Rhys, hating that she was thirty yards away. But if she ran back over there, she'd likely lose her connection.

"Is he conscious?"

"No. Please send someone. We're at the lookout. It's miles back down the trail. I can probably—"

"I've already dispatched a chopper. Help is on the way, ma'am."

Hanna slumped, relief flooding her. "Thank you."

"I'm going to stay on the line with you until they get there. Are you near the patient?"

"No. I had to move to get reception. I can see him, but he's not moving."

The dispatcher asked for all of Rhys's personal information and any medical information Hanna might know. She informed them of his family history of sudden heart attacks and that she knew he was on preventative medication.

"That's good information. Do you have any aspirin on you? Or energy potions?" she asked.

"I'm not sure. I don't, but I don't know what's in his pack." Hanna started to run back over to Rhys.

"Okay, if you find an aspirin, give him one. If he's having a heart attack it will help. If you find any energy herbs or potions, try to get him to ingest some."

"I'm on it," Hanna said. "If I lose you it's because I'm out of range."

"I understand. I'll call you back and will keep trying if we get disconnected."

"Thanks." Hanna reached Rhys's discarded backpack. She didn't find an aspirin, but she did find the champagne, and seeing it instantly made her hate herself. Why had she hesitated when he'd asked her to marry him? Why had she doubted him and their future? Dammit! She dumped the contents of his backpack out, finding a bottle of energy potion.

"I found a potion," she said into the phone, but she didn't wait to find out if the dispatcher was still on the line. She scooted over to Rhys. His eyes were open, and he was blinking up at her. "Hey, you," she said softly. "I need you to swallow some of this potion."

"Hanna?" He frowned at her. "What happened?"

"You passed out, baby. Now come on. I need you to swallow as much of this as possible." She lifted his head and rested it on her leg, then she held the bottle up to his lips.

He tried to sit up further, but her hand on his chest kept him mostly immobile.

"I've got you. Just drink now."

He wrapped his hand around the bottle and tipped the container. His Adam's apple bobbed as he dutifully swallowed the liquid.

She ran her had through his hair and clutched at his arm. "Just relax, Rhys. Help is on the way."

He frowned, and this time when he moved, he did push himself up. His color had returned, but his breathing was shallow, and she feared the worst. Had he had a heart attack? If so, how bad was it? "What do you mean help is coming?" he asked her, his voice sounding a little stronger than before.

"A medical chopper is on the way," she said, returning his items to his backpack.

His eyes locked on the champagne, and he grimaced as he rubbed at his chest again. "I honestly thought we'd be celebrating right now."

"We'll celebrate later," she promised.

His eyes went to her hand and Hanna was painfully aware that she wasn't wearing his ring.

The ring.

Where was it? She frantically scanned the ground. He'd been holding it when he'd fallen. Her throat got tight as she started to use her hands to search the dirt for the ring.

"Hanna?"

"I have to find it, Rhys." The sound of chopper blades

sounded in the distance. She glanced up and felt a rush of relief and gratitude. They'd know how to help him. And suddenly, even though it pained her that they might have lost the ring, it didn't matter. All she cared about was making sure Rhys was okay. She reached out and grabbed his hand, holding on tight. "They're almost here."

"Okay." He leaned back against the rock they'd been standing on when he'd proposed and closed his eyes.

Hanna stood and waved her arms toward the chopper, making sure the pilot saw them. And then the next thing she knew, the helicopter was hovering above them and they lowered a paramedic down to the lookout.

"He's right there," Hanna pointed to Rhys. He was still propped against the rock, but his eyes were open, and he was trying to get to his feet.

"Hold on there, buddy," he said to Rhys. "Let me take some vitals first."

"I'm okay," Rhys said. "I think I just passed out. Maybe it was the altitude."

"He was clutching at his heart," Hanna said, her insides still jumpy at the memory of him falling off the rock into the dirt.

"All right." The paramedic took his vitals and seemed satisfied as he pulled Rhys to his feet. "The heart isn't anything to mess with. We need to get you in and looked at. Are you okay with letting us haul you to the chopper?"

Rhys glanced at Hanna. "Can she come with us?"

"Hell yes, I'm coming," she insisted.

"Sure. We can take you both, but we need you to go up one at a time. Mr. Silver first."

Hanna watched as they hauled Rhys up with a harness and a cable. When it was her turn, the paramedic tried to soothe her and make sure she wasn't going to freak out.

"I'm fine," she said firmly. "I recently jumped out of a perfectly good airplane. This is nothing."

The paramedic gave her an approving nod. "Okay then." He gave his crew a thumbs-up, and the cable started to haul her up to the chopper. Just as she was lifted off the ground, she spotted the rose gold piece of jewelry.

"Oh my god! There it is." She pointed and said, "My ring. It's right there to the left of your foot. Please, it's my engagement ring."

The paramedic frowned as he scanned the ground. "I don't—"

"Two steps to your left, right by the boulder! It's right there!" Frustration seized her, and she wanted to strike out at something, anything. How could he *not* see it? The cable kept pulling her up, and she was certain the ring would be lost forever. But then the paramedic bent down, brushed away a section of the dirt, and closed his fingers over something. She just prayed it was the beautiful rose-gold treasure Rhys had tried to give her. If she got it back, she intended to put it on her finger and never take it off.

"Welcome aboard," one of the flight crew said as they maneuvered her into the chopper. Once she was free of the harness and cable, he handed her a headset.

"Thanks," she said, already scanning for Rhys as she put the headset on. She spotted him lying on a table against the wall. He was already hooked up to a few machines that she didn't understand.

"Sit over here," the paramedic said, pointing to a bench. "As soon as we get Harvey in, we're taking off.

Hanna took her place against the wall and closed her eyes, trying to stave off the sudden emotions that were overwhelming her. She'd mostly held it together while waiting for the chopper, but now that the adrenaline was wearing off, she was in real danger of breaking down.

Her phone that she'd shoved in her pocket vibrated against her leg. She pulled it out and noted a text from an unknown number. *The chopper should be there. Have a safe trip to the hospital and good luck to you and your fiancé. You did great.*

That was it. The tears fell silently down her cheeks. She was so overwhelmed that she didn't even notice Harvey had taken a seat next to her until he was pressing the rose-gold ring into her hand.

She let out a little gasp, shoved the ring on her left hand, and then flung her arms around him. "Thank you!"

He patted her awkwardly, and through her headset she heard him say, "You're welcome."

She let go and turned to face Rhys and found him staring at her. She raised her left hand, pointed to the ring, and mouthed, *yes*.

CHAPTER 21

"*H*anna?" Millie Silver ran into the waiting room of the hospital wearing dusty jeans and a dirt-stained T-shirt. Her dark hair was pulled back in a low ponytail, but wisps had come loose and now framed her pinched face.

"Over here." Hanna stood and strode over to Rhys's mom.

The woman grabbed Hanna and pulled her into a hug. When she pulled back, she grasped Hanna by the arms, holding on tightly as she asked, "How is he?"

"I'm not sure. Stable, but other than that, they haven't told me much. They wanted a relative."

"Right." Millie let go of her and took a step back. She scanned Hanna, then her own body, and she grimaced. "I'm so sorry, dear. I was gardening when I got the call. I didn't think to clean up."

Hanna glanced down at herself and almost laughed. She was covered in dirt too, but it had nothing to do with gardening. She'd soiled her outfit while sitting on the ground with Rhys and searching for the ring that was now safely on her finger. "This is from the hike, not you." She squeezed Mrs. Silver's hand. "But we do make a fine pair."

"We do." She glanced over at the nurse's station. "I'm going to go see if I can get an update. I'll be right back."

Hanna stood there just watching her go. The wait before Millie had arrived had been pure torture. Since Hanna wasn't immediate family, they'd been vague on Rhys's condition, and it was eating her up inside. She just needed to know if he was going to be okay. *Please, gods, let him be okay,* she prayed.

A doctor appeared and led Millie down the hall. When they disappeared from her view, Hanna slowly turned and made her way to the restroom. After using the facility, she stared at her disheveled reflection as she washed her hands. Dirt was smeared across her cheek, and her curls were windblown, no doubt from the helicopter ride. She was a total mess.

Her phone beeped, and Hanna scanned the message. It was Clay checking in. She tapped back, *No news yet.*

His reply was instant. *Abby's on her way.*

She doesn't have to do that, Hanna replied.

Too late. Hang in there, Hanna. I'm sure he'll be all right. He's far too crazy about you to give you up just yet.

Guh. You're making me cry.

Sorry. Chin up.

She shoved the phone back into her pocket, washed her face, and did her best to tame her wild mane. When she studied herself in the mirror a second time, she still thought she looked like a hot mess, but at least there wasn't dirt on her nose. Sighing, she went back to the waiting room and sat down.

"Miss Pelsh?" A nurse called. "Is there a Hanna Pelsh here?"

Hanna popped up out of her chair. "Yes?"

"Your fiancé is ready to see you now."

~

RHYS'S DOOR OPENED, and he sat up straighter in the bed, anxious to see Hanna. But instead of his gorgeous fiancé, his mother barreled in.

"Rhys," his mother exclaimed as she rushed to his side. "Thank the heavens, the gods, and the angels, too. You scared the bejesus out of me."

"It wasn't much fun for me either," he said, opening his arms for her impatient hug.

Millie Silver threw herself into his arms and nearly squeezed a lung right out of him with her fierce hold. "I was so scared."

"I know, Mom. But I'm here. And Hanna was a rock star. I went down, and the next thing I knew she had a chopper on the way." He could still see her sweet face as she mouthed *yes* in the chopper.

"Speaking of Hanna…" Millie Silver raised one eyebrow and gave her son a piercing stare. "She seems to be wearing quite the piece of jewelry on her left hand. Is there something I should know?"

He chuckled. "Yeah, mom. I took her all the way up to Witchling Peak so she'd have a memorable day. Although, I have to admit, the medical drama was quite over the top."

"And?" She tapped her foot impatiently.

"I asked her to marry me." The words felt foreign on his lips, but they made him grin like a fool.

"I imagine she said yes if she's wearing your ring." Millie put her hands on her hips and waited.

"She did, Mom. But I also passed out and had to be flown to the hospital right in the middle of the proposal, so can we keep it under wraps until I see her again?"

"Sure, of course." She clapped her hands together and let out a tiny squeal.

The door swung open again and the floor nurse walked in. She checked his vitals, turned a knob on one of the machines, and made a note in her chart. "How are you feeling, Mr. Silver?"

"A thousand times better. When can I fly this coop?"

The nurse gave him a patient smile. "The doctor wants to keep you for observation for a few more hours. She'll be in soon to explain."

Rhys nodded and was about to ask if they could send Hanna in when Millie grabbed the nurse by the arm, and with no small amount of glee, she said, "Rhys's fiancée is in the waiting room. Can someone bring her back here? She deserves to be here when the doctor arrives."

Fiancée. Rhys rolled the word around in his head and decided it was the best damned word in the entire dictionary. Hanna was his. Even after he'd made an ass of himself right after the proposal. "Mom, I said not to tell anyone yet."

She threw her hands up. "Hanna deserves to be here when you talk to your doctor! What part of that did you miss?"

"I didn't miss any of it. I just find it amusing you pulled that fiancée card out right after I told you to keep it under wraps."

The door swung open, and Hanna poked her head in the room. "Hey."

"Hey yourself, gorgeous," he said, trying to ignore his heart flopping around in his chest. "Get in here."

She slipped into the room and then just stood there awkwardly as if she wasn't sure where she was supposed to go.

"Come here." Rhys patted the bed. "I need to tell you something."

Her face went white with pure fear, and Rhys muttered a

curse. "Sorry, didn't mean to freak you out. I just wanted to tell you something. Something good."

Hanna walked over to the bed, and Rhys tugged her down as he made room for her to sit next to him. "What is it?" she asked.

He took her left hand in his, eyed the engagement ring, and nearly choked up. But he swallowed thickly and said, "That ring looks really good on your finger. I was wondering what you'd think of a fall wedding?"

She let out a startled bark of laughter. "That's what you're thinking about, sitting here in the hospital bed? When you're going to get me down the aisle?"

"Hmmm. I was also thinking we could have the ceremony at your dad's vineyard. We could serve his wine instead of champagne and maybe the new ciders the brewery will be rolling out."

"You talked to my dad?" she asked, searching his eyes as if she wasn't quite sure what to make of what he was saying.

"Sure." He pulled her in closer until her head was resting on his shoulder. "Yesterday. I asked him for his blessing."

She tensed slightly as she sucked in a breath of air. "What did he say?"

"He basically said he'd support whatever you decide and then wished me luck." Rhys stroked her arm. "He was great. Your mom, on the other hand, she's not so wild about the idea."

Hanna sighed heavily. "I don't know what's gotten in to her. I could've sworn that, up until recently, she was all for us getting together. I don't know what changed. Remember when you came in to the café when she was trying to set me up with Chad?"

"Sure. I saved you from a blind date you didn't want to go on," Rhys said.

"Right. And she seemed so happy about it. I could've sworn

she was dancing a jig in the back room. But then after our date, she just wigged out. I don't get it."

Rhys pressed his lips to the top of her head and remembered something her dad said. "Your father thinks this all has something to do with Charlotte. He said she's been having a hard time lately and it's not really about you and me."

"I saw her at the cemetery the other day," Millie said from across the room.

Both Rhys and Hanna jerked their heads in her direction.

"Sorry, didn't mean to eavesdrop." Millie wrinkled her nose. "I think you guys might've forgotten that I'm here."

"I didn't forget, Mom," Rhys said. "It's fine."

"What was my mom doing at the cemetery?" Hanna asked, sitting up straighter. "She never goes there. It's too hard."

"Purging, I think." Millie sighed. "Rhys knows I go a couple of times a month. I like to keep Keith's grave tidy," she said, referring to her late husband. "This was the first time I've ever seen her there. She was pretty upset. Crying like one does when they are heavily grieving. I wasn't sure if I should leave her alone or not, but I couldn't let her suffer in pain like that, so I just went over and held her. I whispered a few of my own truths about the pain of loss, and after a while, she calmed down."

Hanna's hand flew to her open mouth, and tears shone in her dark eyes. "My poor mom. I've never seen her like that before. Not even right after we lost Charlotte. She cried of course, but she never broke down like that."

"Maybe it was time," Millie said. "I don't have the details, and I wouldn't talk about them even if I did because that's not my story to tell, but I suggest you both give her the benefit of the doubt. We all know she loves Rhys. Whatever her reasons, I'm sure there is pain driving her actions right now."

"I wish I'd been there," Hanna said.

Rhys hugged her closer and realized he didn't feel even an ounce of resentment toward Mary Pelsh. They'd all been through a lot, and he figured that eventually she'd come around. She'd loved him once before; she could get there again. "Maybe you should find some time to talk to her. Try to get her to open up about Charlotte."

"Maybe."

The door flung open, and the woman in question rushed in. "Rhys! Oh, my goodness. Are you okay, honey?"

CHAPTER 22

"*I*'m all right, Mrs. Pelsh. I promise," Rhys said, while Hanna stared at her mother. What was she doing there? Hanna had called her parents once they'd made it to the hospital, just so they knew she was okay before the rumors started swirling, but she hadn't expected either of them to come to the hospital. She was perfectly fine.

Mary ran over to the opposite side of the bed from Hanna and flung her arms around Rhys. "I'm so sorry. I thought I'd jinxed you with all of my morbid what-if talk." She glanced up and met Millie's eyes. "I was so scared for you, Mil. How are you holding up?"

"I'm fine," Millie Silver said kindly. "We're just waiting for the doctor to give us an update."

Was she there for Millie? They had been friends for a very long time.

Mary wiped away a tear and nodded. Then she turned to Rhys and took a deep breath. "I'm so sorry, honey. I was so mean yesterday. You didn't deserve that."

Hanna's heart nearly pounded right out of her chest. What

had she said to him the day before? If it was anything like what her mother had said to her about Rhys, she was going to be livid. But Mary was apologizing at least.

"Thank you for saying that," he said, his voice a little rough as if he had a lump in his throat. Hanna squeezed his hand, silently sending him support as he added, "We've all said things we don't mean. It's all right. We can just forget it."

Mary glanced at Hanna. "Are you all right, honey?"

"I am," Hanna said softly. She studied her mother, wondering if she should tell her of their pending engagement. If Mary went off again about Rhys's potential medical problems, Hanna would lose it on her. But she had shown up here and apologized to him. Not to mention the fact that Rhys said he'd already told her parents he was going to ask her to marry him. Her mother wasn't stupid or clueless. She had to know Hanna would say yes. He was the only man she'd ever loved. After a moment, Hanna bit her bottom lip and held her left hand out. "Rhys asked me to marry him."

Mary's eyes welled again, but she sucked in a halting breath and said, "He's a lucky man to be getting my baby." Her smiled trembled with emotion as she peered at Hanna's hand. "That ring is gorgeous." She leaned in, looked closer, and frowned. "But I think it might need to be cleaned."

Hanna let out a chuckle that turned quickly into a laugh. Tears born of a jumble of emotions stained her cheeks as she remembered the paramedic finally finding it in the dirt right before she was hauled up to the chopper. "Yes, Mom. It does. We're thinking a fall ceremony in the vineyard."

Mary averted her gaze, pretending interest in her clasped hands as she said, "That would be lovely. Your father will be thrilled."

It wasn't the over-the-top excited reaction Hanna might

have previously expected, but it was good enough for now. "Mom?" Hanna asked.

Mary Pelsh lifted her chin and patted away the tears rolling down her cheeks. "Yes, honey?"

"Everything is going to be wonderful even if it's messy. No matter what happens, I will never regret this choice." Hanna spoke her truth with loving confidence. "I hope you can trust me to know my own mind. That I'd rather spend one year loving Rhys with my whole heart rather than deny either of us this precious gift." She turned to him, barely holding back her tears. "I pray with everything I have that we'll grow old together right here in Keating Hollow, but if that dream is taken away from us, I won't regret us being together for a single second."

His eyes shone with so much love Hanna could almost feel it wrapping around her. "Me, too, love. Me, too."

"Oh god," Millie said, clutching her chest. "That's beautiful."

"She's right." Mary sent her daughter a small knowing smile and then moved to Millie's side. The two women hugged each other and instantly burst into tears.

"Now you've done it," Rhys said.

She chuckled. "Look who's talking? That was one heck of a proposal, Silver. A little dramatic, don't you think?"

"It worked, didn't it?"

"Yes, it did," she whispered and snuggled into him. "But as much as we both seem to enjoy a challenge, let's not try to top that one, okay?"

"Deal."

The door swung open again and Healer Snow strode in. "Well, hello to my two favorite patients. I hear we've had quite the excitement today."

Hanna tried to get up from the bed, but Rhys kept a surprisingly tight hold on her, keeping her firmly in place. She gave him a look, indicating he should let go, but he just shrugged and kept his arm around her. Hanna rolled her eyes but couldn't help secretly loving his possessiveness. After the events of the day, she was happy to stick to him like glue.

"We did," Hanna said. "I think Rhys was just trying to impress me with a helicopter ride."

He snorted. "You're the one who called them."

"Damn straight. And I'll do it again if you decide to pitch head first into the dirt right after proposing."

"Hmm, very interesting. Proposing? Do you have news?" Snow asked.

Hanna held up her hand and beamed.

"Congratulations. Very exciting, indeed." She glanced back at the two moms who were still holding on to each other. "Mary, Millie, it's good to see you both, too. How've you both been?"

"Doing well," Mary said.

Hanna knew that wasn't true. Even though her mother had accepted that she and Rhys were together, something was totally off with her, and it was going to take more than one conversation to resolve it.

"Good until today," Millie said. "When I got that phone call..." Rhys's mom swallowed and then cleared her throat before whispering, "It was just like reliving that day all over again."

Mary wrapped her arms around Millie, holding her close. "He's okay, Mil. Just breathe now."

Their shared, raw pain made Hanna's heart ache.

"But I can't stop thinking about what if," Millie said so quietly Hanna almost didn't hear her.

"Now don't go borrowing trouble," Mary gently scolded her. "I've been doing that enough for both of us."

"Mary's right," Healer Snow said. "In fact, once you all hear what we've discovered, I think you'll all rest quite a bit easier."

That got Hanna's attention. "About Rhys?"

"Yes." She turned to the man in question. "Perhaps we should talk in private first?"

"Is it about my heart?" he asked.

"Yes. And your diagnosis," the healer confirmed.

"Then there's no need to talk in private. I'm just going to tell everyone here whatever you say anyway."

"All right." Healer Snow flipped open the folder she was holding. "First things first. The issue today had everything to do with the new medication we put you on. It caused your blood pressure to drop to unsafe levels. It's a known side effect that presents in less than two percent of patients. If you hadn't gone hiking, it likely wouldn't have been a problem and we would've caught it at your checkup and taken you off it immediately."

"So he didn't suffer a heart attack or anything like that, right?" Millie asked.

"That's correct. He just passed out from low blood pressure, altitude, and exertion. The IV and energy potions we've administered have stabilized him. His heart is fine."

Hanna felt all the tension ease from her body. Rhys was fine. He hadn't been dying on top of that lookout.

"Am I going back on the old medication?" Rhys asked.

Healer Snow shook her head. "No. In fact, you don't need any medication at all." She walked over to the bed and pulled up a stool to sit next to him. "When you came in today, we pulled blood and ran a bunch of tests. The technician saw something that was interesting and asked me to come take a look. It turns out that the gene you carry, the one that puts you at risk for sudden cardiac arrest, has a slight mutation that was missed the first time you were tested."

Hanna's spine started to tingle, and she knew this was going to be a big deal. "What does that mean?"

The healer glanced around at everyone in the room. "It means that Rhys's risk of a cardiac event is less than five percent. No meds are needed. All we need to do is keep an eye on the heart and make sure there aren't any abnormalities. I'd say a full exam once every six months for the next few years, just to make sure the medication itself hasn't caused any changes, and then after that, it's just an annual exam."

Everyone was completely silent as they absorbed the news. Hanna was tempted to ask the healer to repeat herself, but she couldn't get the words out. She was too shocked.

Rhys had frozen beside Hanna, and even though she couldn't seem to speak, she was able to squeeze his hand in both of hers. Finally, he sucked in a breath and said, "Are you saying there's only a slim chance I'm going to fall over from a sudden heart attack?"

"That is what I'm saying." She grinned at him. "I ran the test three times myself, just to make sure. Your chances of an incident are no better or worse than most men of your age."

"Whoa." He turned to Hanna. "Did you hear that, love?"

"I heard," she whispered, her voice hoarse with emotion. "I heard every word." Her tears spilled over, and she grinned up at him. "I guess you're stuck with me for the next sixty or seventy years."

His bright gaze searched hers, and she felt the depth of his love all the way down to her toes. He fingered the ring he'd given her. "I hope you were sure when you said yes, Han. Because you're stuck with me now."

"I'm sure," she said. "I've never been more certain of anything in my life."

"Thank the gods." He leaned in and brushed his lips over

hers. "Think the parents will leave now so I can give you a proper kiss?"

Hanna laughed. "Probably not. But kiss me anyway. They'll just have to deal."

Rhys grinned then tilted his head and kissed her so thoroughly that by the time he broke away, her head was spinning.

"Well, I guess we won't have to wait too long for grandchildren," Millie said.

"Oh, gods. They're still here?" Hanna said, cheeks flaming with heat.

"Afraid so." Rhys's chest rumbled with amusement. He tore his lips away from Hanna's and spotted Healer Snow talking to his mother. "Hey, Snow. When am I getting sprung from this place?"

"Any time you're ready, Rhys. All your vitals are normal now," she said.

"Thanks." He turned his attention back to Hanna. "Ready to take me home? I think we need to celebrate."

Hanna giggled and slid off the bed. "Your place or mine?"

"Whichever's closer."

CHAPTER 23

Talking about going home was one thing. Deciding who was going to take them was entirely another. Rhys wrapped his arms around his fiancée and waited while his mother and Mary debated who was going to get to drive them home.

Mary insisted her vehicle was roomier and probably more practical. Millie claimed she lived closer to both Hanna and Rhys and it just made more sense for them to go home with her. Besides, she had leftovers at home she could pick up and give to them. Mary said she'd stop and get them something from Hanna's favorite place there in Eureka, and on and on they debated.

"Hey! You've been sprung," Abby said as she strode toward them.

"Abby, thank the gods," Hanna said, pulling her into a hug. When she released her, she said, "Please tell me you're our ride out of this joint."

Rhys waved at Abby, relieved to see her. The thought of spending the next forty-five minutes with either of their mothers was giving him a headache. He gestured to the bickering duo. "We can't ride with either one of them or the other will probably combust with envy."

Abby glanced over at them and winced. "Wow, they've really worked each other up into a lather, haven't they?"

"You have no idea," Hanna said.

"I've got this." Abby squared her shoulders and trotted over to the women.

"I feel a little bad," Hanna said, glancing up at him. "They were so worried, and now we're ditching them."

"Nah. We're just practicing self-preservation." He winked at her. "Besides, if we get into either of their cars we're going to be grilled for every detail of today. I don't know about you, but it's not something I want to share with either of them. Not now. And not before we have a chance to talk about it."

Hanna frowned. "Talk about which part?"

Rhys hadn't intended to bring it up so soon or in the hospital, but he hadn't forgotten her reaction when he'd asked her to marry him. She'd been completely freaked out, and he needed to know why. He was more than willing to accept her yes, the one she'd given him in the helicopter, but before they moved forward, he needed to understand what happened. "The part right after I asked you to marry me before I passed out."

"Um… okay." She tore her gaze away, but not before he saw the fear flash in her beautiful eyes.

"Hey, gorgeous. Don't do that," he soothed, needing her to know he wasn't trying to pick a fight. "I just want to understand what happened there. Whatever it is, we'll be fine. I promise."

Before she could answer, Abby strolled up, a self-satisfied smile on her face. "I'm a genius!" She brushed a strand of her long blond hair back behind her ear. "I told them we needed to go get your Jeep from the parking lot where you left it. They were both a little disappointed but understood you're gonna need your wheels."

Rhys groaned. "Damn. I forgot about that." He slipped his arm around Hanna, making sure she knew he wasn't pushing her away by bringing up what happened at the clearing. "Can we at least get food first? I'm starving."

"Sure, we can get food. But don't worry about the Jeep. Just give me the keys and I'll handle it. Let's get going. I'm sure you're exhausted."

Hanna threw her arms around Abby. "Thank you," his girl said. "Don't tell Faith, but you're my new best friend."

Abby chortled. "It'll be our little secret."

"OKAY GUYS," Abby said as she pulled into Hanna's driveway. "Need anything else before I go pick up Olive?"

"I'm good," Rhys said. He ran his fingertips over his girl's arm. They were in the back seat as if Abby was their chauffer, but he hadn't wanted to be physically separated from her after their crazy day. He was thankful Abby didn't seem to mind.

"Hanna? How about you?" Abby asked, glancing back at her.

"We've got food and a new lease on life. What else do we need?" Her smile was forced, and Rhys wondered if Abby picked up on it also.

"Cool." She spun around and started texting on her phone.

Nope. She hadn't noticed. Or else she was pretending. Rhys leaned forward. "Thanks for everything, Abby."

"My pleasure. Where do you want your Jeep delivered? Here or your place? Clay and Drew are going for it just as soon as I take them the key."

He glanced at Hanna. "Here?"

"Sure." She dug around on the floor gathering their backpacks.

"Got it." Abby said.

Rhys handed her his key, grabbed the Chinese takeout, and then climbed out of the car. Hanna joined him, and they both waved as Abby sped off down the road.

"This isn't how I imagined the day going," Rhys said, giving her a crooked smile. "I had big plans for those pools on the way back down the trail."

Hanna let out a soft chuckle. "I bet you did."

"Come on." He tugged her toward her front door. "Let's eat. And then I'm hoping you'll let me hold you for a while."

"If you still want to," she muttered.

He definitely heard her, but he let it go... for now. The last thing he wanted to do was talk about this in the front yard. He wanted to be inside her house where he could soothe all her ruffled feathers and make sure she knew he loved her no matter what. As they climbed her steps, he asked, "Got your key handy?"

"It's not locked," she said with a shrug. "Keating Hollow has its advantages."

He turned to meet her gaze and stared at her as if he could see all the way to her soul. "It certainly does."

"Rhys," she whispered and pressed her palm to his cheek. "Sometimes I just don't understand what you see in me."

"I see everything, love. Your heart, your fear, your compassion, your talents, all of it. And you see *me*, too. Always, even when I'm trying to hide from you. It's why we fit. Don't you understand that yet?"

She bit down on her bottom lip and furrowed her brow.

He pressed two fingers over the creases in her forehead and smoothed them out. "Don't look at me like that. It's the truth. Now come inside. I'm starving."

"All right."

Rhys opened her door and led her straight to the kitchen. He set the bag of food on the counter and said, "I'll be right back."

After washing up in her bathroom, he strode back into the empty kitchen and got to work on setting the table with plates, chopsticks, and two glasses of iced tea. By the time Hanna reappeared, he'd lit the candles and opened the take-out boxes.

"Hey, thanks. This looks great." She leaned in and kissed him on the cheek. The scent of fresh soap hit him, and he noticed she'd not only washed up, but she'd put on fresh clothes too. He found himself slightly envious since he was still wearing his dirty hiking shorts and T-shirt.

"You're welcome." He sat at the end of the table next to her and passed her the lemon chicken while he dug into the sweet and sour pork. They ate in an uncomfortable silence that was driving Rhys crazy. But he didn't want to talk about this over moo shu pork and pot stickers, and he needed the fuel. So he waited patiently until the last fortune cookie was gone and then started clearing the table.

"I've got this," Hanna said.

Rhys waved her off. "Nah. This is nothing. Why don't you go get that shower I know you're dying to take? I'll get these in the dishwasher and then relax on the couch until you're done."

"Rhys," she said, sounding exasperated. "Stop."

Her tone was so commanding he put the plate back on the table and turned to look at her. "Why?"

"Because you're tiptoeing and that's just... I don't deserve that. I was the jackass here. You laid your heart on the line and I..." She shook her head.

"You what, Hanna? What happened? What went through your head after I asked you?" Now that she'd brought it up, he wasn't going to let it go. Whatever it was, she was clearly bothered by it, and he wouldn't keep acting like everything was fine when it wasn't.

"Dammit." She pushed her hair out of her eyes and sat back down in the kitchen chair.

Rhys leaned against the bar that separated the dining room and the kitchen and waited. He knew her. She'd get it out eventually.

"I didn't know you were going to propose," she said as she stared at the table.

"Is that a bad thing?" He'd wanted to surprise her. He'd wanted it to be the best damn day of her life. Instead it had turned into her worst nightmare. All he wanted to do was gather her in his arms, take her upstairs, and hold her until the sun came up. But that wasn't what she'd accept. Hanna was courageous and didn't need him to hold her together... no matter how much he wanted to.

"It shouldn't have been." She raised her head, and there it was. Her need to face this problem head on was clear in her determined expression. "But my mom got in my head. Her stupid arguments were right there, and I panicked."

He raised both of his eyebrows, surprised. "You mean you were thinking about what your life would be like if my heart gave out suddenly? What would happen to you if you became a young widow?"

"Yes." She didn't elaborate. She just threw her confirmation out there and held his gaze as if she had issued a challenge.

"Okay." He shrugged one shoulder, surprised by how much that hurt. He understood it, but it didn't stop the ache in his gut at the realization she'd doubted if she could walk down the unknown path with him. "Why did you decide to say yes?" He hated to admit it to himself, but a bone-crushing thought occurred to him. He cleared his throat and forced out the one thing he was certain he didn't want to ask but had to. "Did you do it because you thought I was dying?"

"God, no!" She jumped out of her chair and strode over to him. "Don't ever think that, Rhys." Tears glistened in her eyes but didn't fall. "I said yes because I love you. Because when faced with the very real possibility that I might lose you, I was holding on with everything I had. I knew in that terrifying moment that I wanted to marry you no matter what challenges we faced. What I told our moms is true. I want as much time with you as I can get, whatever that means."

"Okay. I believe you. But—" he started, hating himself for picking at this wound.

"No buts, Rhys," she said gently. "I freaked out in a big way, and I was scared to tell you why because we've spent literally years trying to get past that nonsense. At first I was afraid you'd run again, thinking that I need something more than you can give me. Newsflash, I'm a big girl. I can take care of me. I know you know that."

"My reason for staying away has vanished, Hanna," he said, watching her carefully. "I'm not at any special risk anymore. Why were you so afraid to tell me?"

She threw her hands up. "Because, you doofus. I didn't want you to think I'm a terrible person. I need you to know I was never going to leave your side. I just had a momentary freak-out."

Rhys actually laughed. He threw his head back and let the laughter rumble through him.

"It's not funny," she said.

"It kind of is," he said softly as he pushed off the counter and held his hand out to her. "This whole time you were worried I'd think you're a terrible person, and I was worried you were having second thoughts because I wasn't dying. Man, we're some pair."

She blinked. "What?"

He shrugged one shoulder. "If you'd said yes just because you thought I might not make it through the night, then I could hardly hold you to that promise, now could I?"

Hanna clapped a hand over her mouth and giggled.

"See, it's funny." He wrapped his arms around her and smiled down at her. "How about we make a pact to stop assuming what the other is thinking?"

"I can do that. We've never had a problem communicating before," she said.

"That's not exactly true. We've never been great at talking about our romantic feelings. Mostly we've swept those under the rug and just ached for each other. Let's stop that, okay?"

"Deal," she said softly and pressed her head against his chest. "I love you, Rhys."

"I love you, too, Hanna."

They stood there holding each other for a long time, until finally Hanna pulled back and said, "You must be exhausted. Let's get you in the shower and then to bed."

"You don't have to ask me twice."

Hanna slipped her fingers through his and led him upstairs to her bedroom.

He stood in the doorway, eyeing the pretty red poppy bedspread and all of her feminine touches, and yawned so hard his eyes watered.

Without a word, Hanna tugged him to her bathroom, turned the shower on, and said, "Go on. I'll find you something clean to wear."

"As much as I'd like to see your panties, Hanna, I don't think they're going to work for me."

She laughed. "Stop. I'm pretty sure I have some of your old sweat pants and a couple of your T-shirts. Just get in the shower. I've got it from here."

The water was so inviting he didn't argue further. He reached behind his head and pulled his T-shirt off. The door clicked softly behind him, and while he was disappointed that Hanna wouldn't be joining him, he quickly shed the rest of his clothes and stepped into the shower. The water beat down on his fatigued body, making Rhys certain he'd gone to heaven.

He stayed under the hot water for what felt like hours. And when he finally emerged, Hanna had indeed found a pair of his old sweats and one of his favorite T-shirts he hadn't seen in ages. He pulled both on and inhaled that scent that was one hundred percent Hanna. A tiny smile tugged at his lips. She'd been keeping his shirt for herself.

When he finally emerged from the bathroom, he found Hanna sitting in the chair in the corner of her room, fast asleep with a book splayed on her lap. He kneeled in front of her, leaned in, and whispered, "Hey, love. Time for bed."

She jerked awake. "What?"

"You fell asleep in the chair. Ready for bed?"

She glanced from him to the bed and then to the bathroom. "I need a shower first."

"All right." He stood and held out his hand to help her up. Then he led her to the bathroom, turned her shower on, and said, "I'll find you something to wear. Just get in."

She gave him an amused smile. "Is this your way of getting permission to rummage through my underwear drawer?"

"Is that a problem?" He raised one eyebrow in challenge.

Hanna peered past him into her bedroom and then at the shower and the steam already filling the bathroom. "Nope."

"Good." Rhys leaned against the doorframe, waiting.

Hanna pulled her T-shirt off, revealing her sports bra, but when she noticed him standing there, she covered herself with her shirt. "What are you doing?"

"Just watching my fiancée get into the shower. Is *that* all right?"

Her cheeks turned pink, tickling him, but she nodded and went back to the business of undressing.

His girl's movements were slow, meant to torture as she took her time working her way out of her leggings one leg at a time. Good gracious, she was even more gorgeous than he remembered. He'd seen her in less plenty of times at the river or the pool. But this was different. Now she was officially his.

Hanna turned and stared right at him as she slipped out of her sports bra, baring her breasts to him. He sucked in a sharp breath and started to move forward, unable to keep his hands to himself. But Hanna put her hand up, stopping him. "Nope. I'm in desperate need of that shower, and before anything happens with us, *if* anything happens with us tonight, I'm getting in there and cleaning off this dirt."

Disappointment rippled through him, but he understood. And instead of torturing himself further, he nodded and slipped out of the bathroom to find Hanna some clothes. He opted for a silky red pajama set and matching panties and then placed them on the counter in the bathroom, pausing only for a moment to eye the outline of her body visible in the frosted glass of the shower door.

Gorgeous, he thought again as he retreated to her bed and climbed in. He had every intention of waiting up until she was out of the shower and cuddled next to him, but his body was fatigued and his eyelids were heavy. As the scent of Hanna rose up around him, he smiled contentedly and fell into a deep dreamless sleep.

CHAPTER 24

$\mathcal{H}$anna woke just before the predawn light and rolled to her side to watch Rhys sleeping peacefully. The night before when she'd finally emerged from the shower, she'd found him passed out, completely lost in slumber. She hadn't had the heart to wake him after the day he'd had, so she climbed in beside him, curled up on his chest, and sighed when his arm came around her.

It had been the perfect way to end the most imperfect day.

Staring at him now, she wanted to drop kisses on his chest and run her hands over his muscled body, but she refrained. There was no time to luxuriate in him before she had to get to the café. If she woke him now, she'd never make it on time. With a small sigh, she rolled out of bed, grabbed a change of clothes, and slipped into the bathroom. Twenty minutes later, she reemerged to find him still knocked out.

Hanna walked carefully over to his side of the bed, pressed a gentle kiss to his temple, and tiptoed out of the room, closing the door gently behind her.

~

"HANNA!" Faith came flying into Incantation Café, her face lit with excitement. "What the hell, girlfriend? When were you going to tell me?"

Hanna grinned at her friend. "Maybe when you came in for your morning caffeine fix? Who told you?"

"Half the damned town." She pouted. "They totally ruined it for me. But ohmigod! I'm thrilled for you both. It's about time you two got it together! Where's the ring?" She grabbed Hanna's hand and gasped. "Holy sparkles, this thing is gorgeous!"

"Thanks." Hanna smiled so wide, her cheeks started to ache. Ever since their talk the night before, when she confessed her freak-out to Rhys and he absolved her of any perceived betrayals, she just felt happy. A sweet, soul-deep happiness that she hadn't ever really experienced before.

"Goodness, Han. You look like sunshine is just bursting from you." Faith pulled her into a giant hug and whispered, "So, did you two finally do it?"

"Faith!" Hanna pulled back from her friend and shook her head. "Stop."

"So that's a no?" Faith sighed heavily. "What is wrong with you two? You're *engaged* now. Time to get busy."

Hanna rolled her eyes. "Why don't you worry about your own bedroom activities and just let me worry about mine, okay?"

"But yours are about to get *really* interesting," Faith said and leaned on the counter.

"Maybe you and Hunter need to spice things up. Go over to that adult toy shop in Eureka? Pick up a few silicone—"

"Hanna!" Mary Pelsh said from behind her. "That is not the

kind of thing you should be talking about in the café. What's gotten in to you?"

"Oh, crap." Hanna glanced at her mother's stern expression and winced while Faith cackled. "Sorry, Mom. I was just trying to needle Faith because she was... um, getting too personal."

"That's all fine and well, honey, but everyone knows if you're going to frequent an adult toy shop you should go to the one in Arcata. They have a much better selection."

"Wha... what?" Hanna sputtered.

Faith erupted into full blown laughter as she bent over at the waist and gasped for air.

Mary smirked at her daughter and strolled back into her office.

"Holy bells, that was funny," Faith said when she got herself under control. "Who knew Mom had such a strong joke game?"

Hanna shook her head and slipped back behind the counter. "Did you want something, or are you just going to continue to torture me?"

"I need the largest mocha you have and half a dozen chocolate pastries. Or muffins. I don't care just as long as I get my chocolate fix."

"Rough day?" Hanna asked.

"My mom called this morning." Faith shoved her hands in her pockets as all her humor fled and was replaced by a troubled expression. Her mother was a potions addict who was in treatment after accidentally burning Faith's house down a few months earlier.

"What does she want?"

"To make amends. She wants me to come visit so she can apologize in person."

"Didn't she already do that when you and Hunter went to

see her before she cut her deal?" Hanna asked as she steamed the milk for her friend's drink.

"Yes. But now she says she has to make amends for stuff she did when we were kids. She wants Abby, Yvette, and Noel to go, too, but I think that's a pipe dream. Noel won't go for sure. She's still holding on to her anger. Yvette and Abby might. They're more forgiving."

"And you?" Hanna passed her a bag of chocolate croissants.

"I'm probably with Noel on this one." She closed her eyes and gave her head a tiny shake. "I don't want to deal with her. Why does she always call me when she wants to reconnect?"

"Because you're the baby, the one who doesn't remember as much as your sisters. Likely she has less guilt where you're concerned." Hanna gave her a sympathetic smile. "You don't have to take her calls, you know. You don't owe her anything, Faith."

"I know." Faith's shoulders slumped. "But every time she reaches out, I become that little girl who's desperate for answers. I need to know what she wants."

"I'm sorry. I know that's got to be hard."

"It is. But I'll deal."

Hanna finished off the mocha, topped it with a generous portion of whipped cream, and then passed it to Faith. "No charge today. Go back and enjoy the crap out of your busy spa and bask in your success. You deserve it."

"Thank you, Hanna," Faith said, reaching over the counter and giving her another hug. When she pulled back, she dropped a ten in the tip jar and winked. "Later gator."

"Later skater," Hanna said.

The door chimed, indicating Faith's exit just as Hanna's phone vibrated. The call was from Healer Snow.

"Hello?" Hanna said.

"Hanna, oh good. I'm glad I caught you," the healer said.

"We got your blood test back, and I need you to come in to talk about the results. Can you get here this afternoon by four?"

"My results? I thought you just needed to make sure I was right for the drug trial?" Hanna said.

"Yes, that's true. It turns out we have another one that is better suited, but it requires a consult. Do you think you can make it today? Four o'clock?"

"I hadn't planned on driving to Eureka today," she hedged. Hanna was planning a special night with Rhys. If she had to go all the way into town, it meant she might not make it back in time for their dinner reservations at Woodlines.

"Please, Hanna. It's important," the healer said.

A trace of unease crawled up Hanna's back. The trials she'd done so far had been important, she was sure, but she'd never heard that much urgency in Healer Snow's voice before. "All right. I'll be there. Just a consult, not a treatment, right?"

"That's correct. The treatment will be tomorrow if we move forward."

"Tomorrow? Whoa. You're not messing around with this one," Hanna said.

"No, I'm not. I'll see you later today." The healer disconnected, and Hanna stared at her phone, wondering what was going on. Healer Snow had never been that pushy before, nor had she asked Hanna to switch trials at the last minute. She wasn't quite sure what to make of the situation, but as usual, Hanna was determined to do whatever she could to help. If it brought Healer Snow closer to a cure for the autoimmune disease Charlotte had, then Hanna would gladly postpone any plans. Even ones with her gorgeous fiancé.

HANNA HURRIED into the clinic where she normally met with

Healer Snow and rushed over to the receptionist's counter. "Hey, Tai, I'm a little late," she said to the woman behind the computer. "I was supposed to meet Healer Snow—"

"Ten minutes ago," Tai said, cutting her off. She bounded out of her chair and opened the door to the exam room area. "Healer Snow is waiting for you, Ms. Pelsh. Right this way."

Hanna followed the petite woman down two hallways until she came to a stop in front of Snow's office. Tai knocked twice and said, "Hanna Pelsh is here to see you."

"Send her in."

Tai opened the door and gave Hanna a tentative smile.

"Thanks," Hanna said.

"Good luck," the receptionist said as Hanna passed by.

"Good luck? For what?"

Tai stammered.

"Never mind." Hanna strode in and shook the healer's hand before taking a seat. "Thank you for all you did for Rhys. I can't tell you how relieved we all are. It's like you gave him a new lease on life."

Healer Snow muttered a curse.

"What?" Hanna asked, straightening her spine. "Something's wrong. Is it Rhys? Was there another mistake? What don't we know?"

"It's not your fiancé, Hanna. He's fine. Or at least he should be as long as he takes care of himself."

Hanna leaned in and said, "Just tell me whatever it is You're making me really nervous."

"All right." Snow straightened her shoulders, met Hanna's piercing stare, and said, "It's your bloodwork, Hanna. You're not eligible to participate in any more trials as a baseline."

"What does that mean?" Hanna frowned.

"It means you can't be the control case anymore because

your blood test indicated that you've developed the same autoimmune disease that your sister had."

Hanna heard the words but wasn't sure she could process them with all the sudden buzzing that was going on in her head. "It's a mistake," Hanna said. "It must be."

"It's not," The healer said. "I double-checked. Triple-checked. Sometime between the last trial and this one, you've developed the early stages of Charlotte's autoimmune disease. I'm sorry, Hanna, but the science is clear. Are you all right?"

No. Of course she wasn't all right. Hanna felt like she was floating right out of her skin. *Autoimmune disease.* The two words just kept rolling over and over in her brain. Weak, fragile, breakable. That's how the two words *autoimmune disease* made her feel. And in that moment, she really wanted to punch someone.

"This isn't fair," Hanna said.

"It never is," the healer agreed.

"So now what?" Hanna demanded, not sure who she was angry at. The healer? Herself? Charlotte? Tears burned hot in her eyes, and she forced out, "You need my blood for some other trial?"

"No, Hanna. You're the subject of the trial. We have what we need. We just need you to come back tomorrow so we can administer the antibodies."

"Yeah, sure. Tomorrow." Hanna stood. "What time?"

"Ten a.m."

"Got it. I'll be here." She felt her tears finally start to fall, and she angrily brushed them away as she ran to her car. Just when her life had finally fallen into place, she learned the worst possible news. Her body was cold, and her limbs felt numb as memories of Charlotte's sickest days flooded back to her. She saw Charlotte pale in her bed, unable to move; vomiting after yet another experimental treatment; guzzling two extra energy potions just so she'd have the vitality to spend the evening out with her friends or her boyfriend, Drew. And then there was the morning when they found out that Charlotte had died.

Years of fear and pain slammed into Hanna, and she let out a low, guttural sob and steered her car toward Keating Hollow.

CHAPTER 25

"*M*om?" Hanna stumbled through the front door of her childhood home. Her eyes burned from the tears she'd shed on the way back to Keating Hollow and her chest was tight with fear.

"Hanna?" Her mother started down the stairs. "What's wrong honey? Is it Rhys? I thought he was fine. Did something go wrong?"

"It's not Rhys," Hanna rasped out, her throat raw.

"Then what, honey?" Mary wrapped her hands around her daughter's upper arms and really studied her. "Are you hurt?"

She shook her head. Hurt wasn't the right word. Devastated? Shocked? Gutted? Any of the three would cover the emotions seizing her insides. But as she opened her mouth to speak, the words wouldn't come out. Instead she flung her arms around Mary and sobbed.

"Oh, Hanna, baby. Whatever it is, we're going to get through it," her mother whispered as she ran a light hand down her daughter's back and gently rocked her as if she were a toddler. "It's going to be okay."

"What's wrong?" Walter Pelsh asked as he came in through the kitchen door.

Hanna stared at him, her vision blurry. "Dad?"

"Yes, hon?" He walked over, and Mary released Hanna, letting her father wrap her in his strong arms. "Let it out, sweet girl. We've got you. Whatever it is, we've got you."

Hanna wasn't sure how long she stayed in her father's arms, holding on for dear life. She let his calm wash over her as she pressed her head to his solid chest. His embrace warmed her frozen limbs and made her feel safe even if she knew it was only an illusion. She knew what was waiting for her. And it was a damned nightmare.

"I'm going to go make some hot chocolate," Mary said. "Whatever this is, we clearly need reinforcements."

Hanna didn't know why, but her mother's statement made her laugh. Hot chocolate was her mother's answer to everything. It always had been. And that one bit of normalcy made her just a little stronger. She sucked in a deep breath. "I have something I have to tell you both."

"Want to go to the kitchen?" Walter asked her.

Hanna nodded, steeling herself against the pain she was going to cause both of her parents.

Walter wrapped an arm around her shoulders and guided her into the kitchen. Mary had already put a box of tissues on the table along with a plate of snickerdoodles. The smallest whisper of a smile tugged at Hanna's lips. If there was one thing she could count on, it was that her mother was always prepared for a meltdown. She couldn't remember when the house hadn't been stocked with fresh baked cookies and the fixings for hot chocolate.

Hanna took her regular seat at the kitchen table and reached for the tissues. Her face had to be a mess, but it was

COURAGE OF THE WITCH

the last thing on her mind. How was she going to sit at this table and rip her parents' hearts out? Another sob formed in the back of her throat, and her breath halted as she tried to suck in air.

"Whatever it is, we're here for you," Walter said, taking his seat beside her and wrapping her hand in his.

Mary, who'd set the hot chocolate in motion with her air magic, hurried over and sat across from Walter. "Where's Rhys, honey? Should he be here?"

Goddess above. She should call Rhys. This affected him, too. She just didn't have it in her to do it. Not yet. Still she nodded because last night she'd made a promise that they'd be honest and communicate with each other.

A small voice in the back of her mind said, *He doesn't deserve this. You can't marry him now.*

She closed her eyes and shook her head, trying to dislodge the destructive thought.

"Hanna?" Her mother asked. "Is that a yes or no?"

Hanna's eyes popped open, and she squeaked, "Yes. He should be here."

"I'll call him." Mary reached for her phone, rose from the table, and walked into the other room. Hanna was glad. She didn't want to hear the worry in her mother's tone as she summoned him. Glancing at the clock, she grimaced. He was probably at her house, waiting for her at that very moment. Their dinner reservation was in ten minutes. It was then she realized she'd left her phone in her car. No doubt he'd already been trying to reach her to find out where she was. She lowered her head and rested it on her arm. This day was a mess.

"He'll be here in ten minutes," Mary said as she entered the room. Then she muttered a curse and rushed over to her hot chocolate operation. The milk had exploded on the stove without her there to monitor it.

"I'll be right back," Hanna said, rising from her chair. She knew she was a mess and wanted to at least try to put herself back together before Rhys arrived. She took her time in the bathroom, washing her face and pressing a cool washcloth to her eyes, and she didn't come out until she heard the front door open and close, followed by the rumbling of voices. Rhys was there. It was time to face the music.

Taking a deep, fortifying breath, Hanna let herself out of the safety of the bathroom and headed back to the kitchen.

Rhys popped up from the chair that her father had previously occupied and hurried over to her. He pressed his palm to her cheek. "What happened, love? What did the healer say?"

"Healer?" Mary gasped out. "Is that where you were today?"

Hanna glanced over Rhys's shoulder and nodded very slowly. She'd forgotten that she'd left Rhys a message that she had to run to Eureka to see Healer Snow.

"Hanna?" her mother's voice rose. "What did she say?"

How was she supposed to say the words she knew they all needed to hear? She wasn't sure she could get her mouth to work correctly. Instead, Hanna met Rhys's eyes and tried to silently share all of her truth with him. He knew her deepest fear. They all did. But if anyone could read her mind, it was him.

"Jesus," Rhys said on barely a whisper as he searched her watery eyes. "The healer found something in your bloodwork, didn't she?"

Hanna nodded, and one tear slipped down her cheek.

He pulled her into a fierce hug. "We're going to get through this, love. I promise."

"What did she say, Hanna?" her mother asked. "What exactly did she say?"

"Mary," Walter said softly. "Give her a minute."

Hanna pulled back from Rhys just enough to look up into his dark eyes. There was pain reflecting back at her, but nothing that looked like fear. It was enough to fortify her. If Rhys was by her side, she could get through this.

"Let's sit," Hanna said and led Rhys back to the table.

Mary blew out a breath, rolled her shoulders, and then calmly walked over to the counter where the hot chocolate was lined up. She grabbed the whipped cream, sprayed a generous helping on each one, and then brought the four mugs over to the table using a tray. The fact that she wasn't using her magic told Hanna that she was shaken. They all were.

Once Hanna had the mug in her hands, she met Rhys's eyes and said, "I've developed the same condition as Charlotte."

Her mother let out a sharp gasp, but her father only reached across the table and squeezed her hand.

Rhys rested his hand on her thigh and asked, "What does Snow recommend?"

"I need to go in tomorrow for some sort of treatment."

"What time?" Mary asked.

"Ten." Hanna took a long fortifying sip of the hot chocolate. The sweetness hit her tongue, and she took a moment to savor the richness. It tasted like love and all the goodness her parents brought to her childhood even in the face of horrible circumstances.

"I'll get someone to cover us both," Mary said. "If I can't, we'll just close for the day."

"Mom, you don't—" Hanna started.

"Hanna, I'm going. It's not up for discussion." Her mother's tone was final. She got up, leaving her mug on the table before she disappeared into the other room.

"Dad," Hanna said, turning to her father. "Keep a close eye on her okay? I know she's in crisis mode, but I'm worried about later when this really hits her."

Her father's hand tightened on hers. "She's strong, Hanna. You don't need to worry about her. She'll move heaven and earth to do what needs to be done. You know that."

She did know that. But she also knew that everyone had a breaking point, and having to relive this nightmare might just be the straw that broke the camel's back for Mary Pelsh. "Just... take care of her."

"I always do," he said gently. "Now, what do you need from me? Reassurances that we'll get through this? Or do we just need to go out in the back field and blow off steam? I can have the tractors up and running in minutes."

Gods, her father was a treasure. She had no idea how he could take in the day's devastating news and then suggest doing donuts on the farm tractors. But he had. He'd been that way with Charlotte, too. With every terrible piece of news that came along, he was there to offer something different from despair. Some of her most memorable moments from her childhood were after a particularly trying day at the healer's office. Her favorite was the day her dad took them to the local race track and paid for them to get rides with professional drivers. Now that she looked back on it, her dad was probably the reason she was fearless.

"I love you, Dad. Let's go check out the tractors," she said, popping up out of the chair, relieved to be able to focus on something else other than her scary health situation.

"Tractors?" Rhys asked.

"It's time to make the donuts, Silver," Hanna said, pulling him out of his chair. "I hope you don't mind a little mud. Springtime down by the pond is always fun."

"Donuts?" he chuckled. "You're not talking about the ones at the café are you?"

"Nope."

Walter draped his arm around Hanna. "Come on, kid. Let's go show your fiancé how it's done.

CHAPTER 26

*H*anna threw her head back and laughed as she watched Rhys turn his tractor in a circle, spraying mud all over her father's ride. They were in the field farthest from the house, down by the pond they used to use as a swimming hole when Hanna was a kid. There were a lot of good memories in that field. And this was going to be another one.

Still laughing, Hanna set the speed of her own tractor and let her foot off the clutch. The tractor shot forward, and with one quick turn of the wheel, Hanna coated her father's tractor with her own spray of mud. The entire exercise was silly and freeing and exactly what Hanna needed.

The moon was high in the sky, illuminating the field and bouncing off the pond. It was a gorgeous night but the wind had started to pick up, and it didn't take long for Hanna to get chilled. Caked with mud but in higher spirits, the trio finally put the tractors away and headed back to the house. Once inside, Hanna cleaned up in one of the upstairs bathrooms, while Rhys took the downstairs, and her father disappeared into the master.

Once Hanna was reasonably clean, she emerged and headed back toward the stairs. But just as she passed Charlotte's old room, she heard the soft muffled sobs of her mother. She poked her head in and felt the crushing weight of grief hit her, just as it always did when she spied Charlotte's old room. It had eventually been turned into a guest room, but there were still signs of Charlotte everywhere. The painting she'd done in high school hung over the bed. She'd stenciled the closet doors with a gorgeous tree of life depiction. And there were inspirational quotes, all of them gathered by her sister, in picture frames set out around the room.

Hanna didn't say a word as she slipped into the room, crawled onto the bed, and wrapped her arms around her mother. Whatever panic Hanna was feeling, she imagined her mother felt it at least two times over. It must've been torture to stand by not one but two daughters in the same medical crisis and be unable to do anything to help.

"I love you, honey," Mary said. "You're going to conquer this. I know it. The gods wouldn't take both of you from me."

Hanna wasn't so sure that was the case, but she nodded anyway, giving her mother the comfort she craved.

"I owe you such a big apology," her mother sniffled as she handed her a folded piece of parchment.

"What's this?" Hanna asked, taking the paper.

"It's a letter Charlotte wrote to the universe. I found it a few weeks ago when I was purging some old boxes in the attic. I started watching Marie Kondo and figured it was time to let go of some things. But then I found a box of Charlotte's and… it nearly broke me. It's been so long since I let myself go back there. And when I did, I don't know, it was like a damn broke and I lost my mind. This letter is the reason I was so negative about Rhys. But dammit, I was so wrong. Look at him. He's your rock."

"He is my rock," Hanna agreed and again felt the twinge of uncertainty. Was it fair to let him walk this path with her? She knew what it meant to have this disease. It wasn't at all the same as a heart condition that could suddenly and unexpectedly take the life of a loved one. This would mean a slow deterioration. Lots of bad days albeit with good ones sprinkled in. It was a mental challenge as well as a physical one, and it wouldn't be easy.

"What's that look, Hanna?" her mother asked softly. "You're not having second thoughts about Rhys, are you?"

Damn. How was it that her mother had the ability to read her mind? She sighed. "I just don't want to put him through what's coming. I love him too much for that."

Mary pressed her lips into a thin line. "That's his choice, baby, not yours, and you have to let him make it. Just like you wanted to make your own choice regarding his health challenges. How did you feel about him pushing you away?"

"I hated it. But now at least I understand where he was coming from."

"I doubt you do. I doubt either of you understand." She wrapped her arms around her daughter and patted her shoulder.

Hanna tilted her head and eyed her mother in confusion. "What's that supposed to mean?"

"It means you're probably protecting yourself from seeing him in pain. You love him, Han. You don't want to be the cause of what makes him ache with sadness. And he likely didn't want to live with the knowledge of the kind of pain he might eventually bring to you and any children you have."

"What's the difference? Either way we're both trying to protect ourselves and each other."

"The difference is if you're trying to protect yourself, you're not trusting the other person to be the one they want to be. Love is messy, baby. And just because you push someone away, that doesn't mean they stop loving you or hurting when you're hurt. But you already know that. I've known it, too. I just forgot it for a while." She nodded to the note in Hanna's hand. "Read that and you'll understand why I said the things I said. Mother's aren't always rational."

Hanna glanced down at the letter. It was in her sister's flowery handwriting.

DEAR UNIVERSE,

Today I learned my condition is getting worse. It's likely I won't live to see my dreams come true. But I want to put them here, shout them out to you in case there's still a shred of hope. All I've ever wanted in this life is to love and be loved. I know I've been lucky in my short life. I have had a great love in Drew. There is no better family than mine, and I have the best friends that a girl could ask for. So it might sound selfish when I ask that you let me live to see my wedding day and the day my first child might be born. I don't need riches or a fancy career, though I'd love to share more of my art with the world. All I want is what my mom has—a family that comes before everything else.

I know that's asking a lot considering my circumstances, so I'll add that if it can't be me, let Hanna's dreams come true. Bestow upon her a great love, a life full of adventure, and the freedom to choose her own path. She always was one for going her own way. I admire her and am sorry I likely won't be here to watch her thrive.

That's it for now,
Charlotte

. . .

HANNA MET her mother's watery gaze. "I don't understand. I already have what Charlotte asked for. Why would you want me to not be with Rhys?"

"Because, honey. I wanted at least one daughter to have it all. I wanted that great love to last a lifetime to make up for what Charlotte lost." She shook her head. "It probably doesn't make sense to you, but I just wanted you to experience what she couldn't. It's not right. But grief is never rational."

Hanna stared at her sister's words and started to feel like the luckiest person in the world. She *did* have everything Charlotte had wished for her... and more. But now she had her sister's challenges, too. "Mom, I think it's time we stopped wallowing."

Mary looked down at her daughter. "I wasn't aware that we were wallowing, honey. I'd say we're still adjusting and trying to find our way forward."

"Okay, fine. But I'm done being sad. I have a life to live, and I'll be damned if I stop just because of this diagnosis. Charlotte never let it get her down. I'm not going to either."

Her mother's lips curved into a smile. "You're right. She didn't."

Hanna slipped out of her mother's embrace and got to her feet. "I'll see you at the clinic tomorrow?"

"We'll both be there," Mary said, all evidence of her tears gone.

"Good. Now go be with Dad. He'll need you to keep him from falling apart after I leave." Walter was great at being strong when he needed to be. It was in the quiet moments that life caught up to him.

"I will. Tell Rhys..." She frowned as if trying to choose her words. "Just tell him we're here, whatever he needs."

"I will." She kissed her mom on the cheek and went to find her fiancé. It was time to go home.

She found him in the kitchen with her dad. They were talking quietly, but as soon as she entered the room, they clammed up. There was no doubt in her mind that her father was educating Rhys on what to expect going forward. He'd probably been testing him, but judging by the determined look on Rhys's face, he was not fazed.

"I'm ready to go home," she said to Rhys.

He quickly rose from the table. "Okay. I'll follow you. Yours or mine?"

"Yours," she said, loving that there was no question that they'd be spending the night together.

Walter got up and hugged his daughter. "Your life is not your sister's, Hanna girl. We don't know for sure what comes next, and your path hasn't been walked yet. Remember that before you go making any big decisions. Hear me?"

She did. "Loud and clear, Dad."

"Good girl." He kissed the top of her head. "See you in the morning."

She hugged him again just for good measure. And then instead of getting into her own car, she climbed into Rhys's and let him take her home.

RHYS FELT like he hadn't taken a deep breath since he got the call from Hanna's mother that he needed to get to the Pelsh residence as soon as possible. The tractor shenanigans had helped a tiny bit, but he couldn't shake the feeling that he was drowning. That he was barely treading water and the life he'd finally carved out for himself would be gone in the blink of an eye.

He'd never really thought that Hanna would get sick. He'd always assumed it would be him. And now that the tables were turned, he wanted to knock the crap out of himself for pushing her away for so long.

What a jackass he'd been. There was no way he'd give a moment's thought to leaving her side. Whatever time they were given, he'd cherish it, and her, until the very end.

"Come here," he said, his voice rough with emotion. They'd just walked into his house on the hill, and he couldn't wait one more minute to hold her.

Hanna didn't hesitate. She dropped her purse in a chair and flew into his arms. She was out of tears, but he wasn't. His eyes were damp as he ran his fingers down the back of her neck and whispered, "I love you, Hanna. You know that, right?"

"Yes." Her answer was simple, but the emotion in the one word wasn't. The rough sound gutted him, and he hugged her tighter.

"I'll be by your side every step of the way? You know that, too, right?"

"I do now," she said and gave him a tentative smile.

He raised one eyebrow. "You weren't sure?"

"Well..." She stepped out of his embrace and wrapped her arms around herself. He wanted to pull her back and keep holding her, keep her safe, but he instinctively knew she had something she had to say. And she needed to do it without him invading her space. "I admit that I finally understand why you kept pushing me away before."

"I was wrong," he said flatly.

"I know." She reached for his hand and held it in both of hers. "My mom and I had a good talk tonight. She apologized for her behavior again, by the way."

Rhys shook his head. "She doesn't need to keep doing that. I get where she was coming from."

"I don't," Hanna said mildly. "I mean, I understand why she said what she said, but I don't get it at all. Not in here where it counts." She pointed to her heart. "This whole time, all I've ever wanted to do was love you. Do you think I'd trade away my sister in order to not suffer the pain of losing her?"

"No, of course not." The question was ludicrous, and he didn't even have to think about it.

"How about you? Would you have wanted a different dad?"

"Gods, Hanna." He closed his eyes. "Of course not. Why are we having this conversation? I thought we were past this?"

"We are. Mostly." She pushed up on her toes and gave him a kiss on the corner of his mouth. "It's just that tonight, after I heard the diagnosis, I started to doubt if you should stay with me, and I needed to hear how ridiculous that sounds when we apply it to those we love. I want to be like Charlotte and keep living my life to the fullest. And that includes marrying you."

"You're damned right it does," he said, nodding.

"Good. We're on the same page."

The tightness in Rhys's chest eased, and suddenly he could breathe again. He hadn't known it, but it was obvious now that he'd been afraid she'd step back from the life they were getting ready to build together. Hearing her say she still wanted to marry him had been exactly what he needed. "We definitely are," he agreed.

"There's something else I don't want to put off any longer," she said, her cheeks turning pink as she reached for his hand and glanced toward the stairs.

He raised both eyebrows and flashed her a smile. "And what might that be, gorgeous?"

Hanna lifted her gaze to his, lifted one eyebrow of her own, and said, "I think it's time you made love to me, Rhys. You know, make sure we're compatible in the bedroom before we get too far into this."

Rhys let out a bark of laughter. "*Before we get too far?*" He reached for her, lifting her effortlessly into his arms. "Honey, we're in so deep a back hoe couldn't dig us out of this. But, sure. Let's go find out just how compatible we really are."

She giggled as he bounded up the stairs two at a time then strode into his room and tossed her onto the bed. He climbed over her, covering her body with his, and once his lips found hers, all of the laughter stopped. Rhys's heart thundered against his ribcage, and his love was so big, so fierce, that he thought he'd burst from it.

Hanna reached up a trembling hand and pressed it against his chest. "I can feel you everywhere already, Rhys."

Her sweet words filled all of his empty spaces. "Good. Because you've already invaded every part of me. I love you so much."

"I love you, too," she whispered. And then all talking ceased as they came together as one.

CHAPTER 27

"Good morning, Hanna, Rhys," Healer Snow said as she strode into her office. "Thank you for clearing your schedules and coming in so quickly."

"Sure," Hanna said, clutching Rhys's hand so tightly she was afraid she might be cutting off his circulation.

"I have some exciting news—" Snow started.

"I don't actually have Charlotte's disease?" Hanna asked, cutting her off.

Healer Snow grimaced. "I'm sorry, Hanna. That's not what I was going to say."

Hanna let out a nervous chuckle. "It was worth a shot."

The healer sent her a sympathetic smile. "As I was saying, we've had a significant breakthrough in treatment for autoimmune diseases. It's lucky that you've been supplying us with your blood for so long in our trials because it means we've actually been working on a cure using *your* blood cells. And the antibodies we have now come directly from your DNA. It's a huge plus for you."

"What does that mean?" Hanna asked. "Do I have some sort

of higher chance for a cure because you used my DNA or something?"

"That's exactly what I mean. You're an exact match. If we can duplicate what we've tried in the lab, then this can be an actual cure. It will be the first time we've managed to reverse this disease instead of just stall it."

Hanna blinked at her, not daring to hope she'd heard her correctly.

"Cure?" Rhys said. "Is that realistic or just a hope?"

"It's realistic all right. In fact, I'm so sure it's going to work that I've already started working on guidelines for those at risk for this disease." Healer Snow's eyes were bright with excitement. "I think we're going to make history here, Hanna. And it's all because you cared enough to keep coming back here for ten years, doing whatever you could to help us learn more about this disease."

"I... um, is this what the next trials were going to be about?" Hanna asked, confused that she was just hearing about a possible cure now.

"Yes, sort of. We were going to try to duplicate what we've been working on already. Remember, before you didn't have the active markers for the disease, so we couldn't test our theory. But then last night after you left, we got to work in the lab and, hallelujah! Success."

Rhys's fingers tightened around Hanna's. "Obviously there aren't any guarantees." They all knew that. "But what are the chances this works?"

"That's a good question. We obviously can't know on an untested treatment, but if I were a betting woman, I'd be laying it all on the line." She grinned at them. "And all we do is administer the IV that includes the antibodies while a healer specializing in Healing Hands makes the magic happen."

"That's it? What are the risks?" Hanna asked.

The healer shrugged. "Not many. Just the usual stuff like a reaction to the antibodies, which is unlikely since you were the original source. And then the risks associated with the healer's magic, which is more art than science."

Hanna glanced at Rhys, feeling both elated and skeptical. "This sounds too good to be true."

"Maybe. But when it comes to magical healing, isn't that always the case?" he reasoned.

"Charlotte tried more than a few of these miracle cures," Hanna said, desperate to not get her hopes up. "I just don't want to go into this with unreasonable expectations. I know what it feels like to think 'this is it' when it couldn't be further from the truth."

Rhys eyed her. "Are you saying no to the treatment?"

She shook her head. "No, that's not at all what I'm saying. I think I'm just trying to process this. Yesterday I was envisioning days of being bedridden, and now I'm being told I could walk out of here with a cure. It's… a lot."

Healer Snow cleared her throat. "Okay, let me clarify a few things. The treatment won't be a one-shot deal. We'll need at least three appointments and maybe up to five, but we'll know after today's treatment if it's even working. When we talk about cures, that means remission and regular screenings. Then if we manage to keep it at bay for a few years, that's when we can say you're cured. Think of this as taking one step at a time. Today might be one small step, or it could be a giant leap. We won't know until we try."

Hanna took a deep breath. "Okay. Let's do it."

"Wonderful." She reached across the desk and shook both of their hands.

"Healer Snow?" Hanna asked.

"Yes?"

"Do you think someone could explain all of this to my

parents? They're out in the waiting room. I'd do it, but I'm not sure I completely understand, and after all they went through with Charlotte…"

"Say no more. I'll have my intern fill them in while we're prepping for the procedure. Follow me."

Rhys and Hanna both stood, but before she could follow the healer, Rhys pulled her into his arms and said, "Good luck."

She pressed her lips to his and whispered, "I hope it doesn't wear me out too much. I had plans for us later."

He chuckled as his eyes glittered with desire. "So did I."

"Hanna? Are you ready?" Healer Snow called from the door.

"Yep." After giving Rhys one last kiss, she spun on her heel and followed Snow into the hallway.

"ARE YOU COMFORTABLE?" Snow asked Hanna.

She was lying on what could only be called a surgical table. The motorized table had thick plastic pads and was positioned in the middle of the room with three large spotlights overhead.

"Comfortable enough," Hanna said.

"Good. We're going to hook up the IV, and then the other healer is going to come in."

"Okay." Hanna closed her eyes, exhausted from the day before. It had been an emotional one, followed by a long night of making love to Rhys. Their time together had been slow and sweet and so full of love she thought she'd burst from the enormity of their connection. It had been wonderful.

And then they'd woken deep in the night, hungry for each other, and that time had been raw with need and full of desperation to be one with each other, to own each other's souls. It too had been something wonderful that they'd both needed. She'd woken in his arms and honestly couldn't remember a time when she'd been so happy and yet so scared of what the day would bring. And maybe that was why she was having such a hard time believing this could work. Life was never that tidy. She just wasn't sure she could trust it. But she was damn sure willing to try.

"Hanna?" a woman asked. "Is that you?"

Hanna's eyes fluttered open, and she spotted a familiar face. "Luna? What are you doing here?"

The pretty blonde smiled down at her. "I'm the Healing Hands tech. Basically I'm going to try to promote healing within your immune system."

"I didn't know you worked here, too." Hanna was blown away by the fact the new massage therapist was here to basically save her life. Although, hadn't she helped Faith heal her sprained ankle? Suddenly Hanna felt a lot more optimistic about the procedure.

"Only part-time. What I do is pretty specialized, and it can take a lot out of me. It's why I'm also working at A Touch of Magic. I need the hours."

Hanna reached out and touched the other woman's hand. "Thank you for being here. I don't know why, but your presence is making me feel a lot better about this."

Luna smiled down at her. "Thank you. That means a lot. I'm happy to do whatever I can."

"Hanna? Are you ready?" Healer Snow asked as she walked into the room and scanned the IV machine and heart monitor.

"I guess so. What do I do? Just lay here?"

"That's pretty much it," Luna said. "It's really not much different than a massage. You let me know if you feel anything strange or are uneasy with anything I do. Otherwise, just lie back and relax."

"Relax." Hanna let out a nervous chuckle. "Sure."

"Don't worry, Hanna. I've got this," Luna whispered.

Hanna took a deep breath and let it out, but she was tense and there was no hope of relaxing.

"I'm starting the IV now, Hanna," Snow said. "As soon as the drip starts, Luna is going to work her magic. Any questions?"

Hanna shook her head as a chill rippled through her. Shivering, she wrapped her arms around her body, trying to maintain a small bit of warmth.

"Don't worry, Hanna. It's just the IV drip. My magic will warm you," Luna said.

"If you say so," she said, her teeth chattering. Hanna's head started to spin, and her stomach rolled. "Oh, god," she moaned and turned on her side, afraid she was going to vomit.

"Turn the lights down," Luna commanded.

The harsh lighting dimmed, but still the IV burned through her veins, and sweat popped out on Hanna's forehead and the back of her neck.

"Make... it... stop," she said on a moan. Her head was pounding, and Hanna suspected she was a moment from a migraine.

"I've got you," Luna said, pressing her hand to Hanna's forehead. Her palm was cool, but the tingle of warm magic glittered over Hanna's scalp, calming the headache.

"Thank you," Hanna whimpered, still clutching her stomach. She started to rock, feeling as if she was going to come right out of her skin.

"Slow the IV drip," Luna ordered. "It's too much, too fast."

Hanna couldn't tell if they obeyed her order or not. All she knew was that she was freezing and bile was rising in the back of her throat.

Luna's hand moved to her neck, the tingling magic a balm against the ice-cold sensation streaming through her body.

"Hang in there with me, Hanna. We're going to get through this."

Hanna listened to Luna's soothing voice and concentrated on her hand working its way down to her shoulder and her bare arm. Warmth started to thaw the bone-deep cold that had gripped her from the inside out. Her breathing became less ragged, and when Luna gently turned Hanna onto her back, Hanna went without resistance.

"There we go. It's working now, right?"

Hanna opened her eyes for the first time since the IV had started and stared Luna straight in the eye. "Keep talking."

Luna nodded, pursed her lips, and then said, "I had a puppy once. Her name was Star. She was tiny. You know, the type that fits into a purse? She was a cross between a shih tzu and a poodle. My foster mom called her a shihzypoo and put her in sparkling collars. That's how she got the name Star. Anyway, Star and I were inseparable. She slept in my bed, followed me around the house, and I, in turn, lavished her with so much love she had no idea she was a dog."

"I had a dog once," Hanna said. "Her name was Willy."

"*Her* name was Willy?" Luna said with a laugh.

"Wilhelmina. Like the modeling agency."

"Ah, makes sense. Did you want to be a model?" Luna asked her.

"I am a model sometimes," Hanna said. "Just not for an agency. I didn't want to leave Keating Hollow."

"I can see why," Luna said and whispered, "Turn onto your stomach for me."

Hanna did as she was told, barely noticing that she was no longer cold.

Luna pressed her hands to Hanna's shoulders, and this time instead of soft tingling magic, heat poured into her muscles, making them feel like they'd been turned to liquid. The sensation repeated over and over as Luna worked her way down Hanna's back. It was intense and wonderful and terrifying all at the same time. Hanna's mind was complete mush. She didn't know if she hated what was happening or if she loved it. But one thing was for sure, Luna was pumping her body full of her intense magic. It had to do something, right?

"Tell me more about Star," Hanna said, her muscles so relaxed at that point she might have slurred her words.

"Star. What a wonderful little pup she was. I took her everywhere in a little mesh case. She was the first being who ever loved me."

Hanna turned her head and blinked at her. "The first?"

"Yep. We were together for nine months before I was placed in another home. I still miss her." Luna suddenly froze, and her mouth dropped open. After a moment, she blew out a breath and started to run her hands down the back of Hanna's legs. "I'm sorry. I don't know why I said any of that. I think our connection must've broken down both of our barriers."

After that, Luna didn't speak except to give specific instructions on how Hanna should position her body. But it was fine. The chill, the nausea, the headache—they had all vanished, and Hanna felt nothing but warm and relaxed. Luna's magic had seeped into her, and Hanna was starting to feel as if she was floating.

The lights flipped back on, and Luna pulled a thick blanket over Hanna before she stepped back. "You're all done," she whispered. "How do you feel?"

"Wonderful," Hanna said, knowing deep in her soul that, somehow or another, Luna had just saved her life. It wasn't a wish or even a hunch. She knew. It was the type of certainty that had only happened twice in her life. The first was when she knew before anyone else that her sister was gone. The second was when her dog Willy went missing and Hanna had a premonition that the pup had been picked up by animal control and was in a shelter in Garberville. She had no reason to have known either of those things, but she had. This was the same feeling.

"Good. That's how it's supposed to work." She turned to Healer Snow, and they talked about the IV drip and how to improve for the next round.

Before Hanna knew it, Luna was gone and Healer Snow was drawing a vial of blood. "We'll get this tested and call you later today." She handed the vial to one of her assistants. "You can get up now."

Hanna sat up slowly, expecting to be lightheaded, but not only did she feel fine, she actually felt like a million bucks. "Holy hell. That woman is like a drug."

Snow smirked. "If only we could bottle her gifts, right?"

"If only," Hanna agreed and followed Snow back to an exam room where she got dressed. When she walked out, Snow was waiting for her.

"You did well today, Hanna. I'll call you later today after we've analyzed the results, but either way, we need you back next week to do this again. Make sure you make an appointment on the way out."

"Will do." She shook Snow's hand and headed out to find Rhys and her parents.

"Hanna!" her mother cried when she spotted her. "How'd it go?"

"Perfect. Snow is going to call with the blood test results later today, but I'm certain they will be clear."

"How can you be sure?" Rhys asked her.

She smiled serenely and patted his arm. "I just am. Everything is going to be just fine now."

Mary narrowed her eyes at her daughter. After studying her for a moment, she nodded as if satisfied. "Good, because

I'm counting on you to keep up your end of the catering at the café. Orders keep coming, and there's no way I can do it all. We'll need to schedule..."

Hanna's mother continued to rattle on about all their future plans for the café while Hanna hugged her dad and held on to Rhys's hand. Everything truly was fine now, and Hanna couldn't wait to start the rest of her life with the people she loved most.

CHAPTER 28

*R*hys tucked Hanna's hand in his and led her down the path near the magical river. They hadn't said much in the car on the way back from Healer Snow's office. Rhys wasn't sure what to say. Hanna was certain the procedure had worked. Not just certain, dead certain. Like it was a done deal. Rhys didn't share her confidence. He wished he did, but how could she trust so blindly in a feeling? He didn't get it. But he sure as hell wasn't going to contradict her about it. Snow would call soon enough, and then they'd know.

"How about October?" Hanna asked him.

"What about October?" He bent at the waist and plucked a wild daisy and slipped it behind her ear.

She smiled up at him, her eyes sparkling with so much life, it nearly took his breath away. "For the wedding. My dad says he'll be bottling his Sauvignon Blanc in late September. That means we'll be able to serve his wine, and it'll be gorgeous that time of year. We could do a harvest theme with gourds and brooms. Maybe a caldron if we want to get witchy." She laughed. "I could wear a white corset dress with thigh-high lace-up boots. What do you think?"

"I think you should save that outfit just for me, Hanna," he said, brushing her curls out of her eyes. "You don't want a groom who's dragging you into the vineyard to have his way with you on your wedding day, do you?"

"Uh, yes!" She lifted up on her toes and planted a long, slow kiss on him.

Rhys wrapped his arms around her, needing to feel her against him. She was so strong, so full of life, that he couldn't even fathom walking through the world without her. He tightened his hold and buried his face in her neck, breathing in her sweet honeysuckle scent. "Damn, you feel good, love."

"So do you, Rhys." She trailed her fingers down the back of his neck, making a shiver of desire ripple through him.

She pulled back and looked up at him. "I have another question for you."

"Two," he said, grinning.

She laughed. "Two what?"

"Two kids. But I can be talked into three. We'd need a bigger house or a remodel, but we could work it out."

"All right." She nodded as if this wasn't the first time they'd talked about having kids, as if they didn't have a debilitating disease hanging over their heads. "I don't see an issue with either two or three, but we do need to decide where we're going to live. Your house or mine?"

He shrugged one shoulder. "I don't care as long as I wake up beside you every day."

"How about we do a pro-con list?"

"Okay. Your place is closer to town. Less commute," he said.

"By what, seven minutes?" She laughed. "Keating Hollow isn't exactly the traffic juggernaut of the bay area."

"True, but if we keep your place, it's close enough for a nooner every now and then."

Hanna snickered. "Okay, that's a pro for my place. Yours has the better view."

"True, and good running trails right behind it," he added.

"Mine is closer to Faith's. It's a pro for me. Don't know how you feel about it."

"Two for town, one for the house on the hill," he said. "Mine has the better bathrooms."

"And kitchen," she said. "Plus, yours is bigger."

"Bigger isn't always better," he said with a smirk.

"The hell it isn't." She dropped her gaze, eyeing his fly. "Trust me, Silver. You're doing just fine."

"That's good to know." They continued to debate which house they wanted to settle down in until Rhys finally said, "Really, it's up to you, gorgeous. Whichever place you want, I'm on board. Or if you want to sell both and start over, I can be talked into that, too. Like I said, I just want you."

Her expression was full of love as she gazed up at him. "You're wonderful. You know that?"

"You're biased," he said.

"Perhaps. But it's still true. Okay, if it's my pick, I want the house on the hill, 'cause you have that great spa tub in your bathroom."

He chuckled. "You know, we could put one in your place if you—"

"Stop." She held her hand up. "I've made my choice."

"Okay. The house on the hill it is."

"Good," she said. "Let's stop at my place on the way home so I can pack my clothes."

"I've got news for you, Hanna. You're not going to need any for quite a while."

"Oh?" She ran a hand down his chest and moved the other

one to his hip. "I think I could be talked into that. How about we go now and—"

Rhys's phone started to ring. "Hold that thought." He pressed the phone to his ear. "Clay, what's up?" He slipped his hand into Hanna's and started to walk again. "Just hanging out with my girl. Why?... Oh?... Sure. Now?... All right. We'll be there in twenty." He ended the call. "We've been summoned to the Townsend compound."

"For what?" Hanna asked.

"Something about a family meeting and they need our input." He shrugged and tucked his phone back into his pocket.

"Family meeting? What does that have to do with us?"

"I guess we'll find out."

"Looks like a party," Hanna said as Rhys made his way up the drive of the Townsend family home. There were already five other vehicles there, leaving only one spot for Rhys's Jeep.

He parked and ran around to the other side to open her door.

"You know you don't have to do that, right?" she said, even as a smile lit up her face.

"I do it because I want to," he said and moved his hand to the small of her back as he guided her up to the front steps.

"Good answer." Hanna reached for the door knob, not even bothering to knock. She'd been a fixture at the Townsend household for years and supposed when you were best friends with one of the Townsend girls, that was just one of the perks. She strolled right in and called, "Hello! We're here."

"In here," a chorus of voices called.

Rhys felt like he was intruding just walking into the Townsend house, but no one else seemed to mind, so he plastered a smile on his face and waved as they rounded the corner into the large family room. Lincoln Townsend was sitting at the dining room table with Clay Garrison, his son-in-law, and Jacob Burton, Yvette's fiancé. The Townsend sisters were milling around the kitchen, making lattes and serving up desserts. Drew and Hunter, Noel and Faith's significant others, were on the couch, flipping ESPN channels, while kids ran around outside with two small shih tzus.

"Rhys. There you are," Lincoln Townsend called. "Come over here. We have something we need to discuss."

"Sure." He kissed Hanna on the temple and started to move toward the table.

"Bring Hanna," Lincoln added.

"You got it." Rhys turned and offered his arm to the love of his life and then led her over to them.

"Sit," Lincoln said. "We have a proposal on the table."

Clay and Jacob were grinning like fools, and Rhys frowned, wondering where all of this was going. He didn't like surprises when it came to his work life and right at that moment, he had no clue why he'd been summoned.

"What's going on, Lin? How are you feeling?" Hanna asked.

"Excellent, Hanna. Just got word I'm officially in remission." He beamed at her.

"Yes!" Hanna jumped up and ran over to him, giving him a huge hug. When she pulled back, she had tears in her eyes. "I knew you'd beat the big C. Thank the gods and all the healers who stepped up to help you fight this battle."

"And a huge thanks to Faith and Abby. Those two girls have magic hands," he said, beaming at his daughters in the kitchen. "And Yvette and Noel, too, of course. Their support has been endless."

"They are truly wonderful," Hanna said, beaming at Faith.

Rhys looked around at all of them and longed to build the

kind of family with Hanna that Lincoln Townsend had. Of course, Lincoln had done it mostly on his own after his wife split, but look at him now. Rhys had grown up with just his mom, and he wanted his children to have siblings, to have this kind of bond with each other when they were older.

"Rhys," Clay said, standing and handing out bottles of cider to everyone. "There's a reason we summoned you here other than to just celebrate the launch of the cider line."

"The launch?" Rhys asked. That was news to him. Last he heard, they were still deciding if it was going to be a small in-house special offering or if they were going to bottle it and sell it through distributors like they did their beer.

"We've had inquiries," Clay explained. "Yesterday our top distributor rep came in. He said he has clients looking for high quality cider, so we had a meeting about it and we're going all-in on one condition."

"What's that?" Rhys asked, trying to ignore the nerves in his gut. He'd been told they wanted him to head the division, but maybe that had been when they were keeping it a small operation.

Clay turned to Lincoln. "Want to do the honors?"

"Absolutely." Lincoln Townsend stood and said, "Son, we're all very impressed with the ciders you've produced. We also recognize that your inherent magical talents are what makes them so special. With that in mind, I'd like to offer to make you a full partner in the cider division of the Townsend Brewery."

Rhys sat there, speechless.

"What?" Hanna squealed. "Ohmigod, that's amazing." She turned to Rhys. "Say something. Did you hear Lin? They want to make you a partner."

Rhys got to his feet and cleared his throat. "That is a very generous offer, sir. I'm afraid I find myself a little taken off guard. That wasn't something I was expecting."

Lin chuckled. "I imagine it wasn't. But this is a family operation, son. And you're family. It was time to make sure you know that."

Rhys glanced down at Hanna and smiled. "I suppose I will be once Hanna and I get hitched. I know your families are close."

"That's true." Lin rubbed his chin thoughtfully. "But even if you hadn't been smart enough to propose to our girl, you're still family, Rhys. How long have you been working at the brewery?"

"Five years?" Clay guessed.

It was actually six, but Rhys wasn't going to correct him.

"It doesn't matter." Lin waved a hand. "Long enough for us to know it's where you belong."

There was a tightening in Rhys's throat as emotion overwhelmed him. He loved the brewery. The thought of being part owner of the cider operation... it was a dream come true. He swallowed hard and forced out, "Thank you for the offer, Lincoln. You have no idea how much I'd love to be an owner, but I don't have the capital to invest—"

"The product is your capital, son. Without that, we don't have a line." Lincoln smiled. "I've got a contract drawn up and ready for you to look over. Basically, it just says that the Townsend Brewery has exclusive rights over the ciders you produce while you're part owner of the operation. You'll have voting rights when it comes to the cider, and you'll earn a share of the profits. There's more, but you should have an attorney check it out and make sure it aligns with your interests."

Rhys was stunned. Lincoln Townsend was handing him a dream on a silver platter. He had trouble believing that the man in front of him would draw up any contract that would screw him out of anything. Lincoln just wasn't that kind of man. But he knew it was smart to do his due diligence. He held out his hand to the older man. "Assuming my lawyer gives the go ahead, I think we have a deal."

Applause broke out in the kitchen as the Townsend girls showed their approval. Rhys shook Clay's and Jacob's hands, and then Hanna caught him up in a fierce hug.

"I'm so proud of you," she whispered in his ear. "They offered you this because you deserve it. You're amazing."

He hugged her tight and kissed the top of her head, more than a little overwhelmed by the day's news. The next thing he knew, he was pulled outside with Lincoln and Clay as they walked the orchard, talking about apple varieties and harvest schedules.

By the time they got back to the house, the sun was starting to set, and Rhys was anxious to talk to Hanna. He glanced around the living room, and when he didn't see her, he asked Faith if she knew where to find her.

"I saw her go out the front door. She got a phone call, I think," Faith said.

Hope and fear both washed over him, rendering him frozen. Healer Snow had said she'd call today. This was the moment of truth. He took off for the front door and tore out onto the porch.

Hanna stood near the front railing, tears streaming down her face, but she was also grinning from ear to ear.

"Hanna?" he walked over to her, not sure he dared to ask the question.

"It's gone," she choked out. "Luna cured me. No trace of the disease. None. Zero. It's like it never happened. Even my DNA is showing I'm no longer at risk. Rhys, other than the follow-up treatments she wants me to have just to be safe, it's over."

He opened his arms and she flew into them. They stood on

the Townsend family porch, locked in each other's arms, as the sun cast an orange glow over Keating Hollow.

Finally, Rhys said, "October twelfth. That's the day we'll get married."

"Why the twelfth?" she asked, pressing her head to his shoulder.

"Because, gorgeous. That's the day I asked you out for the first time in high school. You remember the harvest carnival?"

"Yes. You asked me to go with you so that you wouldn't have to take your neighbor's annoying kid or something like that."

He chuckled. "It was a lie. I just wanted to take you." He fingered the daisy that was still tucked behind her ear. "You know what I learned at that carnival?"

"That is was unwise to eat both a deep-fried pickle and a deep-fried Twinkie?" He could hear the smile in her voice.

"Yes, but I didn't remember until just now," he said. "I learned that daisies are your favorite flower, that monkeys freak you out, and that Prince was your favorite musician."

She glanced up at him. "You remember all of that?"

"Hanna, I remember it all."

Her eyes shone with unshed happy tears, and he was pretty sure his did too as he bent his head and kissed her.

CHAPTER 29

*L*una Scott smoothed her sundress, took a deep fortifying breath, and walked into the Townsend brewery. It was a Tuesday in mid-May and the pub was closed for a private event—Hanna and Rhys's engagement party. The guest list seemed to have included at least half the town, because the place was packed.

"You're here!" Hanna, looking like a super model in her tight jeans, silky blouse, and red spiked heels, pushed her way through the crowd and grabbed Luna by the hand. "Finally. I wasn't sure if you were going to make it."

"Me neither," Luna said. "I had a walk-in at the spa at the last minute. She was a regular from Eureka who got her appointments mixed up. I just didn't feel like I could turn her away." Luna bit down on the side of her cheek to keep from blurting out that her explanation was a total lie. The truth was she'd taken the booking because she wasn't sure she wanted to attend this gathering at all. Not because she didn't like Hanna and Rhys, she did. Very much. It was just that she was much better one on one than she was in large groups.

"Don't even worry about it." Hanna tugged her over to the bar. "Sadie, can you get Luna a drink? She's been working all day, and I know she needs one."

"Sure. What can I get for you, Maggie?" Sadie beamed at her.

Luna bit back a grimace. Ever since Luna helped Hanna beat her autoimmune disease, Hanna had taken to calling her Magic Hands, or Maggie for short. It appeared that the cringe-worthy nickname was going to stick. Luna hated the name Maggie. It reminded her of a foster mother she'd had who'd been a recovering addict and blamed her "kids" for having to stay clean. She'd been a mean bitch who chain-smoked and smelled of moth balls.

"How about a lemonade," Luna said.

"You don't want to try Rhys's newest cider?" Hanna asked. "It just got the highest marks from the Lost Coast Times. It's up for like three or four awards."

"Uh, okay," Luna said, not sure she should be drinking since she had to work at the clinic in the morning, but one cider wouldn't hurt, right?

"Let her drink whatever she wants to, Hanna," Rhys said with a laugh as he slid in beside her. "Not everyone has to try my cider."

"Yes, they do," she insisted. "That stuff is really freakin' good." She turned her attention back to Luna. "I just want you to taste it. I think it's going to be right up your alley."

Luna couldn't help but laugh at her enthusiasm. "I'm happy to taste it. But just a taste. I need to be sharp for tomorrow."

"I'm on it." Hanna slipped behind the counter, grabbed a bottle of Rhys's cider, and poured it into two glasses. She took the one that was fuller and handed Luna the other. "Drink what you want and pass the rest to me. I *love* this stuff."

"She's our best customer," Rhys said. "Too bad she doesn't pay for any of it." He winked at his fiancée, and she giggled.

Good gracious those two were so sweet it almost made her nauseated. But then so were all of the Townsend sisters. If it hadn't been for her work with the clinic in Eureka, helping a lot of sick people, Luna would've thought she'd stepped right into a storybook. Everything about Keating Hollow was pure, almost wholesome. It was a far cry from where she'd grown up in a trailer park on the wrong side of town.

"Drink. Tell me what you think," Hanna urged.

"Right." Luna hadn't ever actually had hard cider before, not even the night they'd all been in the hot spring down by the river. So she had nothing to compare it to. Trying not to look like a hick who'd just stumbled off the bus from nowhere, she sniffed the liquid the way she'd watched Rhys do a few times before and then took a sip. The crisp, slightly sweet flavor surprised her, and she quickly took another sip, once again delighted by the freshness of it. "Wow. Delicious."

"See. I wouldn't steer you wrong," Hanna said, giving her elbow a light squeeze.

"When you're right, you're right," Luna said, toasting her with her glass of cider.

Hanna grinned. "Listen, tomorrow night is girls' night. You busy? Can you meet us at Yvette's shop at seven? We're going to have cocktails and then kick Wanda's butt at golf cart races."

"Tomorrow?" Luna hedged.

"Oh, come on, Luna. You have to. You have no idea how much fun it is sabotaging someone else's race."

Luna looked into Hanna's very sincere and excited expression and caved. It really was time she got out and socialized. She'd been hermitting long enough. And she just liked Hanna too much to say no. "I'll be there. Seven o'clock."

"Yes!" Hanna raised her glass and danced a little jig. "Yvette

and Noel will be excited to finally spend some time with you."
Rhys started beckoning her out onto the dance floor, and she
waved as she rushed out to meet him.

The DJ put on a high energy swing number, and Luna
watched as the perfect couple launched into a coordinated
dance, complete with lifts and twirls and a whole bunch of
moves that would end with Luna face-first on the floor. Was
there anything they couldn't do? She was so caught up in
watching Hanna and Rhys that she didn't even notice when
someone sat on the stool beside her.

"Hope, is that you?" a strikingly familiar voice said from
right beside her.

Luna felt her blood run cold, and she froze, pretending she
hadn't heard him. Maybe if she didn't turn and face him, he'd
think he had the wrong person.

"It *is* you," he said, sliding off his stool and moving to stand
right in front of her. "My god, I never thought I'd see
you again."

The boy who'd been responsible for the worst day of her
young life, stood right in front of her, his deep, soulful eyes
searching hers.

"Chad," she said, her voice quivering. "What are you
doing here?"

"I live here now. I'm thinking about opening a music store.
What are *you* doing here?"

"I'm a guest of Hanna's." Her throat closed up and she had
to squeeze her eyes shut to keep from crying.

He reached out and engulfed her small hand in his large
one. Regret rolled off him in waves as he said, "I meant what
are you doing here in Keating Hollow?"

"I..." She lifted her eyes to his and remembered with
perfect clarity the last words he'd said to her that night when
he'd shattered her heart. Chad Garber was her first love, and

the one person who knew all her secrets. He was also the one who could ruin her new life in Keating Hollow. She couldn't keep sitting there talking to him. It was far too dangerous for both her heart and her safety.

"Hope?" he said again.

She cleared her throat, pulled her hand from his, and stood. "I go by Luna now."

"Why?" he asked, confused.

"I just like it better," she lied. "It was nice to see you, Chad, but I have to be going. Have a good evening."

With her head held high, Luna strolled out of the brewery and straight to her little Kia Sportage. Once she was safely inside the vehicle, she gripped the steering wheel and forced herself to breathe.

Chad Garber had just walked back into her life, and she was nowhere near ready for him.

DEANNA'S BOOK LIST

Pyper Rayne Novels:
Spirits, Stilettos, and a Silver Bustier
Spirits, Rock Stars, and a Midnight Chocolate Bar
Spirits, Beignets, and a Bayou Biker Gang
Spirits, Diamonds, and a Drive-thru Daiquiri Stand

Jade Calhoun Novels:
Haunted on Bourbon Street
Witches of Bourbon Street
Demons of Bourbon Street
Angels of Bourbon Street
Shadows of Bourbon Street
Incubus of Bourbon Street
Bewitched on Bourbon Street
Hexed on Bourbon Street
Dragons of Bourbon Street

Witches of Keating Hollow:
Soul of the Witch

Heart of the Witch
Spirit of the Witch
Dreams of the Witch
Courage of the Witch
Love of the Witch

Last Witch Standing:
Soulless at Sunset
Bloodlust By Midnight
Bitten At Daybreak

Witch Island Brides:
The Vampire's Last Dance
The Wolf's New Year Bride
The Warlock's Enchanted Kiss
The Shifter's First Bite

Crescent City Fae Novels:
Influential Magic
Irresistible Magic
Intoxicating Magic

Destiny Novels:
Defining Destiny
Accepting Fate

ABOUT THE AUTHOR

New York Times and USA Today bestselling author, Deanna Chase, is a native Californian, transplanted to the slower paced lifestyle of southeastern Louisiana. When she isn't writing, she is often goofing off with her husband in New Orleans or playing with her two shih tzu dogs. For more information and updates on newest releases visit her website at deannachase.com.

Made in the USA
Monee, IL
22 March 2024

55533181R00152